A GODDESS SCORNED

Hera Greek Myths Retold Book Two

Ava McKevitt

SAPERE BOOKS

Also in the Hera Series
Queen of Heaven
Nemesis of the Gods

A GODDESS SCORNED

Published by Sapere Books.

24 Trafalgar Road, Ilkley, LS29 8HH

saperebooks.com

Copyright © Ava McKevitt, 2024

Ava McKevitt has asserted her right to be identified as the author of this work.
All rights reserved.

No part of this publication may be reproduced, stored in any retrieval system, or transmitted, in any form, or by any means, electronic, mechanical, photocopying, recording, or otherwise, without the prior written permission of the publishers.
This book is a work of fiction. Names, characters, businesses, organisations, places and events, other than those clearly in the public domain, are either the product of the author's imagination, or are used fictitiously.
Any resemblances to actual persons, living or dead, events or locales are purely coincidental.

ISBN: 978-0-85495-503-9

For Livi, my greatest source of inspiration.

1: OLYMPIA

The Muses have sung many songs over the aeons, as is their duty. They have visited many poets, musicians, and writers in their visions, inspiring them with tales of heroism and glory, love and companionship, enmity and destruction, but these exaggerated recollections fall far from the truth.

These enchantresses of creativity, these gossip-mongers, relayed my story in a shamefully misleading way. It was in the time of Homer, in the Archaic Age, some seven or eight hundred years before the birth of Jesus Christ when they inspired bards to spread malicious lies about me. I have often chided them for this. In response, they have lamented that Zeus, their father, directs them to say what they do, that seldom is their work original. My youngest brother and husband, the King of Heaven and the Olympian gods, the father of humankind, established civilisation and society but allowed misogyny to fester in his kingdom.

The poet Semonides, a great favourite of Zeus's, wrote a notorious rant on women. He claimed that every woman is by nature a trickster and a harlot, ignorant in everything except how to eat. Moreover, a woman, he said, was a loud and noisy vixen who could not be silenced, even with violence. She is like the sea: unpredictable and dangerous. He did not stop there. Oh no. Then he likened the woman to the sex-crazed, thieving weasel, the vain and lazy horse, or the hideous ape who only humiliates her husband. According to him, there is only one suitable type of woman, the one like the bee, a rare specimen who is hardworking, devoted, and does not talk or even think for herself. He reminded his audience that Zeus created women as a curse to mankind but that Pandora, the first woman, must still take the blame.

Of course, I cannot agree with falsehoods such as these. As the patron goddess of women, marriage, and motherhood, I must defend these insults and tell the truth about the world that Zeus was building. Not even the Muses knew the details of my part in these tales. It is a journey only I can take you on. I do not wish to repeat myself in detail, but I shall start where I left off. And so, as Homer called upon the Muses to fuel his tall tales, I now need only call upon myself for the truth.

Oh, Hera of Olympos; Olympia.

Sing of the never-ending cycle of life, death, and resurrection. Sing of how the seasons were formed, turning over the days and nights between hot sun and cold stars. Sing of the tragic union of love and fire: how lust lay with bloodshed and brought a volcano to erupt; where the ash had settled and love's heart truly lay. Sing of the eternal contest between love and loyalty; of the unwanted, unsought depredation of goddesses' in Heaven and women on Earth, of the bond of sisters and mothers, and how it can be wholly severed but fully repaired, even among the hot-hearted heavenly hosts. Sing of the growth of civilisation; how, with wine, the masses relieved themselves from their daily suffering to the sound of bestial drums with manic movements; and how it came to fail them in resolving their earthly issues. Sing of how even the heavenly ones cannot escape their woes, sorrows that cannot be relieved no matter how much is drunk or danced away. Sing of the Age of Heroes, when cities were still being born from the womb of Mother Gaia; of Theseus and the foundation of Athens with undeniable bravery but immense selfishness too; and of Herakles, the epitome of the perfect man, made known to the world with his birth and unfortunate end. Sing of how I realised what I meant in this world, how the state of matrimony could be justified, and how motherhood could be both a blessing and a curse. Sing of how I became a goddess of life and death in my own right, taking the breath of others into my own fair hands.

The last year had been unbearable for me, as a goddess of family, to be almost entirely without her kin, or at least any relatives that genuinely cared for me. I had my daughters Eileithyia and Hebe, the last of whom was still in the nursery. However, my pride and joy, my two sons, Ares and Hephaistos, as well as the others — Poseidon, Haides, Athena, Apollo, Artemis, Hermes, Demeter, and Aphrodite — were banished by Zeus from Olympos after our uprising against him.

It might have been a success had it not been for Hestia, the eldest of my siblings, who insisted that it was not right or just to engage in such conflict within our own home. I might have forgiven her weakness had she chosen to remain neutral, but she did not. Instead, she took action to thwart us, bringing the matter to Queen Thetis of the Nereides, whom I despised. With the help of a Hekatoncheir, Briareos, Thetis released Zeus from his captivity and restored him to the throne. She wished to supplant me as Queen of Heaven, trying to present to Zeus the idea that she, a common sea nymph, was more suited to being queen than his own Olympian wife. However, he still chose me and sent her home. Briareos was once more cast down into the depths of Erebos.

Afterwards, my family was enslaved for a year to toil in Dardania. While they laboured, Zeus dispensed his special punishment on me: isolation. At least if I had been committed to servitude with my children, I would have had them for company. Even today, I wonder if Zeus knew he was giving me the worst of punishments: to be trapped within the same walls as him with no ally or friend. And so, I went to the Moirai for hope, some glimmer of light beyond this dark void, that I might one day be content in my life. Like any oracle, the three old crones gave me a riddle, saying I would be happy but not in my union. It made no sense: as a goddess of matrimony if I was not content with my husband, how could I ever be happy? What more did I have to take pleasure in than my husband and my children who came from him? I pondered all this with an abundance of time while awaiting my family's return, hoping that when they did, we would once more topple Zeus from his almighty perch. At last, the long-awaited day came.

Murmurings of anticipation and curiosity rippled through the courtiers, who had gathered in the throne room in the palace of Olympos. Feet tapped on the ground with impatience. Heads turned to the golden double doors at the far end of the hall. Necks craned to see who would come through them.

Zeus clenched his jaw. He sat on his throne with a stony expression as he stared at the same doors. I could tell he was bracing himself, preparing to display as much patronising grandiosity as he could muster.

I was sitting beside him on my own royal seat. Before the court summoning, I had received instructions from my husband, via the nymphs, on how I should behave at this assembly: silent, serene, and compliant with whatever Zeus might order. However, I found it challenging to sit still now, knowing my family would soon be in my arms again. This was the moment I had been dreaming of every night for months.

Even though the attention of many was on the double doors, gazes darted every now and then towards me on the dais. I, too, was on display. It had been some time since I had been welcome to join Zeus in public. Over the last year, I had been confined to my quarters, not permitted to be seen by any. It was only at night that I dared venture outside without my husband's knowledge and, even then, under a shroud of invisibility. My punishment trickled into custom: wives were best kept indoors to be observed, away from prying eyes and opportunities for meddling and mischief; the wife became a naturally suspicious and indomitable creature for her husband.

Finally, the doors were opened, light spilling into the dimly lit throne room. Several figures entered. They were covered in sweat and grime.

Hephaistos and Ares flanked the group, pushing the doors open by their great handles, their muscles straining against the weight of the gold. Hephaistos's black hair was matted and mane-like. The scars on his face had multiplied somehow — perhaps he had been beaten for his ugliness. His limp was still present as he approached. Meanwhile, Ares had grown a beard, and his fair hair had been chopped off for selling. I learned later that the slave masters had envied his golden head. Both my sons had been stripped to a loincloth and nothing more. Both had been used as the group's primary labourers, being the strongest, with lashings flayed across their skin, raw wounds that would leave scars for the rest of eternity, and permanent reminders of their year in slavery for betraying their king.

Zeus's daughter Artemis had her arm slung over her twin brother Apollo's shoulder as she limped into the throne room. Fresh ichor trickled from her shaved head, her golden locks gone, while Apollo had a scar down his face and was peppered with scratches from blades.

Athena wore a golden gash on her cheek with bruising rising to her hairline and ear. Ichor trickled from her nose, and her bottom lip was swollen. She had been used as target practice for the soldiers, with arrow wounds on her arms and legs.

Aphrodite, the goddess of love and beauty, also stumbled inside, her tunic ripped to show her lean body beneath. She had been battered, beaten, and bruised, that was for sure. There was discolouration about her neck, wrists, and pelvis. Her long golden ringlets had been hacked off. Dark shadows lay under her blue eyes, which had lost their sparkle. It was not difficult to imagine what had happened to her.

My sister Demeter entered the throne room, bandages wrapped around her feet, her hair untamed. She seemed off-balance and not entirely aware of her surroundings. I later learned that she had not slept for the year she toiled at Dardania. The goddess of agriculture was forced to wander throughout the lands of Phrygia to make the crops grow all year round, without a moment's respite.

My brother Poseidon still wore the remnants of ropes around his feet and hands. His nose was deformed, his skin peeling, with bits of dried seaweed, shells, and coral caught in his long hair, all in a knotted mess. He had been used for digging up shipwrecks and dragging the fleet around the sea to save money on paid sailors.

Haides, my eldest brother, was barely recognisable, with a long, scraggly beard. He, too, was thin and malnourished, with sores about the skin on his face. Yet, besides that, he did not bear any injuries I could see. He glared at Zeus. There was a steeliness in his gaze that the others did not share; the rest kept their eyes on the ground.

My throat went dry. The sight of them filled me with regret and resentment. I looked at Zeus, a smirk in the corner of his mouth, and anger shot through me.

My husband stood up from his throne and spread his arms. "Welcome home, my beloved family. You have been dearly missed. Yet I hope you have learned the true nature of what I have given you here on Olympos, the power you enjoy by my permission, and what awaits should you abuse that privilege. Kneel now and renew your allegiance. Then you shall be pardoned."

They did so, one by one, vowing to never bring force or danger against him again. Afterwards, Zeus permitted them to rise and reclaim their rightful places on their empty thrones, which were arranged on either side of the dais. A silent dread settled over the court as the Olympians took their places once more. Zeus stared coldly around at them all. All sensed that things would never be the same again.

Once the court was dismissed, clean clothes were fetched for them. Food and drink were served to them. Soon, they wanted for nothing but sympathy. Artemis and Apollo embraced their mother, Leto. Ares, Hephaistos, and Athena came to me, kissing my cheek. I strongly resisted the urge to hold them tightly, remembering Zeus's instructions.

After a shouting match with their youngest brother, which could be heard all over the palace, Haides and Poseidon immediately departed for their kingdoms. Poseidon, always the more passionate of the three brothers, soon forgot his anger once he had let it out. Haides, on the other hand, brewed silently. Beneath the earth, one could not know what the Lord of the Underworld was thinking, and it was probably just as well.

As for most of those who remained, their spirits were crushed. All kept their distance from Zeus and remained silent and supplicant, finally beaten into submission. It was despairing to see the depression in their eyes whenever they were in the same room as their king. Any hope of reigniting the revolution seemed utterly hopeless. Aphrodite appeared to be the worst affected. In the days that followed, she mostly kept to her bed and would not receive anyone except for Ares. However, there was one who responded to the situation quite differently.

2: DEMETER

In the weeks that followed Aphrodite approached me while I was sitting with my ladies, dressed once more in her beautiful clothes. Her bright blue eyes were ice-cold as she curtseyed deeply and requested an audience with her queen. Her tone was formal and serious. A tense and awkward silence settled over the scene and, in my heart, a sense of dread and confusion grew.

She led me into a small antechamber where no one could interrupt us.

Once inside, after ordering all the guards away, I stood waiting, warily.

Aphrodite fixed me with a vicious glare. "How could you?"

I stared at her, baffled. "What?"

"How could you condemn me to that lame monster?"

Oh. Hephaistos. Whilst in the pit of my woes over the past year, I had forgotten my promise to my son that he could take the goddess of love for his wife in an apology for my absence during his youth.

Understanding her annoyance, I tried to reassure her. "I understand it has come as a shock, but it is a good match, Aphrodite; you are to marry a prince of Olympos. What is wrong with that?"

"What is wrong with it? Do you recall that I love Ares, with whom I have a daughter?" she demanded.

I raised an eyebrow. "You are not married to Ares, and that has not stopped you from lying with others."

Her hands clenched into fists. "Hera, I do not even know Hephaistos."

"You have the rest of time for that. He has loved you from afar ever since he heard your name," I replied, trying a smile. "He will be forever devoted to you. He will care for you and consider your feelings. He will be a husband few wives could boast of."

Aphrodite scoffed. "If Hephaistos truly cared about my feelings, he would not force me to do something that will make me unhappy. What is more, neither would you."

"Something that will make you unhappy?" I repeated, incredulous. "Do you not see how fortunate you are? He is an honourable person. There is love on his side. Is that not enough for you?"

Desperation entered her beautiful eyes. "No. It is not enough for true love. Whatever Hephaistos feels for me, it is not real."

I huffed. "Hephaistos is willing to dedicate himself to making you happy. You will come to appreciate that and be grateful for it. I am sure you would agree that true love is built over time with effort from both sides."

Her expression dropped. "You do not know how many times I have said that myself. And so, I see now that I am a fool, and you a hypocrite," she hissed, her face contorting into a thunderous scowl. "I will never be able to love him."

"Why not?"

She shrugged. "He is not who I desire."

I shook my head, my patience wearing thin. "Aphrodite, I am sorry this is not what you wanted, but I will not recant what I promised him. Hephaistos spent his whole life hating me. I cannot ruin again what I have just fixed."

She blinked in realisation and then choked on her words. "You mean you are doing this for him without thinking of me? Or even Ares? Does he not matter? He is your son too."

"Ares will not find it difficult to discover new love elsewhere."

Aphrodite stared at me in disbelief. Her voice was quiet. "I never thought you would do this. Never in my life did I think you would treat either of us in such a way."

I shook my head. *What a reaction!* "Love will grow in time if you give it a chance. You have said such things even about my marriage," I reminded her.

"Was I right? Has that happened?" she cried, tears welling up in her eyes. "Do you love Zeus yet? Does he love you?"

Her sudden interrogation shocked me. I did not know what to say.

She took a deep breath to calm herself. Then she looked at me as tears streamed down her face. "How would I know the value of my own advice on love in marriage when it is something I have never known? Now, thanks to you, I never will."

My heart was full of regret. "There is nothing I can do about it now. I have given Hephaistos my word."

"You have handed me over to him like some heifer you bought at the market. Such is your misery; you cannot bear to see others happy."

"Zeus defiled me. The situations are vastly different," I reminded her.

She raised her chin. "You are right. I see that and I pity you, Hera, for Zeus will never care; he will never notice your pain, and you cannot change him."

"I thought you did not know the value of your advice," I spat in return.

Aphrodite bared her teeth in a malicious grin. For the first time in her life, she looked ugly, and a shiver ran down my spine. "I have seen his heart," she growled. "It is rotten."

Zeus gave the match his blessing. To my surprise, when Aphrodite resisted, he ordered her to do it. After that, with the upcoming union now public knowledge, I received a visit that, in hindsight, I should have seen coming.

"Is it true?"

I turned around and saw Ares, my firstborn, standing behind me.

He looked like his normal self now, dressed in his usual garb of a brown cloak and a breastplate, but he seemed weary, weighed down by all that had happened to him. His silver eyes were red from weeping, and his breathing was heavy. The anger drawn across his face reminded me of his father, thunderous and unreasonable.

"Well?" he demanded, his voice catching.

My heartbeat sped up, realising what he meant. "My dear boy, I regret that this has come as a shock, but I made a promise to Hephaistos and I never intended any hurt by it. I just wanted to make him feel part of the family."

"What about my family? Aphrodite and I have a daughter together."

I searched for the right words, my face growing hot. "It slipped my mind."

Ares balled his fists at his sides. "It slipped your mind to ask Aphrodite's permission before arranging her marriage or to consult me on with the prospect of my daughter's mother marrying another?"

"Harmonia is married now herself. She is no longer a child. Besides, if Aphrodite being with others is such a problem to you, why did you not marry her? You had every opportunity."

He splayed his hands in exasperation. "That is not who she is. That is not who I am! Being tied to one entity for the rest of time is impossible for both of us."

Running a hand through his short hair in frustration, he approached me, his eyes imploring. "Mother, this will be a bloodbath if you go through with it. I can cope with Hephaistos having a night with Aphrodite, if it will keep the peace. But it is in no one's interest that they wed, for Aphrodite will never love him."

"You do not know that," I replied, softly. "Marriage is a wonderful thing. It can be happy and fulfilling."

"Yes, for those who want it," he stressed. "Yet can you honestly count yourself among the happily married, to speak about its benefits when you do not feel them?"

I did not have an answer. That is what marriage was supposed to be.

"Mother, I am begging you." He took my hands in his. "This will cause so much pain."

I broke his grip. "Zeus has already given the match his support. To go against it now would be to disobey him. I cannot do that either."

Ares took a step back, staring at me as if for the first time. Then he nodded as he turned away. "No, I did not think you would."

As I walked through the palace gardens on my way back from the spring, carrying a freshly filled hydria, I was thinking deeply about the upcoming marriage of Aphrodite and Hephaistos, what preparations would need to be made, and more. The sunlight of Helios shone from above through the treetops, casting dappled shadows along the pathway before me.

Suddenly, I trod on something soft and spongy. Alarmed, I jumped to the side and saw two serpents on the ground, intertwined amid the leaves. At first, I was anxious that I had brought some harm to them, but as I crouched down to inspect them, a sudden cold fear washed through my veins, and goosebumps appeared on my arms. I caught an unmistakable grey gaze glaring up at me from the eyes of one of the serpents, lightning flashing in its irises, ordering me away.

Sucking in a breath, I stood and hurried away. My heart was beating fast, and my eyes began to sting, realising who I had seen and what I had witnessed. However, I only took a few strides before coming to a halt. It occurred to me that this was a moment I would have once, in darker days, given anything to take advantage of. But the Moirai had given it to me now.

Slowly, I turned around and approached the coiled snakes as they writhed and slithered over each other. Disgust seized me, and my anger flared. I raised my leg and kicked the serpents for all I was worth, lifting them apart with my foot and flinging them into the air. Momentarily airborne, they turned into their proper forms before me.

My husband landed on the ground at my feet, naked and holding a hand to his face. "Hera! What do you think you are doing?" he bellowed.

I was not listening to him. I was not even looking at him. My eyes were fixed on the person next to him, who had just a moment before been wrapped around him on the ground: Demeter. I stared at her silver eyes, her long, wild, dark hair cascading over her shoulders, her whole figure glowing in the sunlight. As I continued to look at her, my knees felt weak. While I had grown used to his mistresses being strangers, mere mortals, Titans or nymphs, I had never imagined Zeus would choose one so close to me, a member of my own family.

Demeter stared back at me, stone cold in her expression.

Zeus cleared his throat, getting to his feet. "Hera, go inside."

I blinked. *Of course.* They were not going anywhere. They certainly were not going to stop, not because of me. At best, they would continue their activities elsewhere. So, my heart hammering inside my chest, I quickly turned around and, keeping my gaze fixed on the palace ahead, left them to resume their treachery.

Demeter found me in the nursery later that day after I had taken Hebe to her music lessons. My sister was dressed now, her hair piled up on her head as it should be. She did not knock but closed the door behind her.

I had been folding Hebe's garments on her bed when I looked up and saw my sister standing there. Once I did, I had to turn away immediately. I put my hand against a nearby wall to steady myself. I had been trying desperately to distract myself all day, but now the problem was here to talk to me.

"I am sorry you saw that. You should not have found out that way. It must have been horrible for you." Her words were sympathetic, but there was no remorse in her tone.

I shook my head, my nails digging into the wall. That was one way to describe it. "Tell me, how should I have found out?"

There was silence. I glanced over my shoulder at Demeter. "Answer me."

She looked at me defiantly. "I do not know, Hera. I do not know what to tell you. However, consider this: you are married with children; you have stability. Some of us have nothing. For centuries, I have been disregarded. Iasion was taken from me at Harmonia's wedding. His child, Ploutus, I could not love. Then Zeus wanted me, and there it was: a chance for happiness."

Trembling, I felt nothing for her tragedy. I could not believe her; she was making no sense.

"I do not expect you to understand," she said. "Know that there is no emotional connection between Zeus and me. It is purely physical."

Did she think that made it any better?

I gritted my teeth. "How long?"

"Since my return from Dardania. I am not trying to usurp you or make your life difficult. I know Zeus will lose interest in me. I am reconciled to that. It is what I would prefer. I do not want a serious attachment."

I slapped my outstretched hand against the wall and whirled around to face her properly. "Then what do you want? What does a common whore want?"

She stared at me, clenching her jaw. "I am not a whore, Hera."

I found myself yelling at her: "Going into the bed of your sister's husband for no other reason than pleasure must be whoring. So, do not tell me you feel left out of the good times! At least if there was something real between you, I could have respected you. Did you have any thoughts for me when you lay with him?"

She lowered her gaze.

My eyes stung. "Of course you did. At least Hestia had the decency to say to my face that she did not support my struggle against him."

Demeter looked up, taken aback. "Hera, I fought for you. I know how much you hate him. That is why I thought you would not mind."

"What are you saying? That is precisely why I mind. I try to get on with my life, to make it bearable. I constantly fight to get Zeus's good opinion while he betrays me with other women." I paused. She knew all this. "What kind of sister are you?"

She did not reply. She just looked away.

I shook my head. This was the last thing I had ever expected. It was almost comical. "You had a lover once and the chance to be a mother, yet you cast both aside. I thought you loved Iasion, but here you are, neglecting his child and jumping into his killer's bed."

Demeter curled her fists. "Do not dare speak that way about him or his son, Hera."

"I dare when you are a hypocrite."

"You know nothing. I came here to say sorry, which I am. I truly regret that this has hurt you. I did not think it would."

Her apology was not good enough. "Yet you do not regret it?"

She hesitated, then shook her head.

I curled my lip at her. "Get out of my sight. Never speak to me again."

She stood her ground for a moment. "Or what?"

"Or I will put you back into Kronos's stomach, for it is where you belong," I growled.

It took us both a moment, but we quickly realised I was being sincere. So, Demeter left promptly without another word.

I do not regret my outburst. Demeter had known my darkest fears and secrets, helped me when I was in need, admonished me for not being more forthright, and fought with me against him. She had been publicly humiliated, scorned, and exiled, like the rest of my family. She, too, had slaved at Dardania for a year, suffering under the worst physical strain. She had every reason to be repulsed by him. Why she wasn't, I could not understand. Perhaps she thought that, rather than fight Zeus, she should accept him, join him, or more — use him. Maybe she thought advances from the King of Heaven were too good an opportunity to pass over. Perhaps he did not repel her as he did me. I found it hard to fathom. Soon I gave up asking. I gave up completely.

3: TETHYS

A hurricane blew over the Great Sea on the night I abandoned Olympos. Torrential rain battered the ground, soaking my dress, but there was no lightning. I stood on the edge of the mountainside, gazing out into the black abyss as the gale howled and screamed. Selene was nowhere to be found in the night sky.

I closed my eyes, took a deep breath, and stepped forward, letting myself fall off the mountaintop, trusting the wind to take me anywhere it wanted. Anywhere other than here. And so, the world watched me drop from Olympos. The rain drummed down as I descended through the cold air. The wind knocked my body every which way, tearing my clothes and tangling the hair around my neck. Finally, I smashed into the sea, and all was black.

My head rang from the impact. Then the icy water invaded my mouth and nose. I did not fight it despite how much instinct told me otherwise. I closed my eyes, ready for whatever these deep waters would do to me. Perhaps it was for the best. Zeus could find his new queen in Demeter, and I would no longer have to endure his infidelity. Instead, I could lie on the floor of the ocean's dark depths forever, with salty water around me, and watch the world drift by, no longer alive yet never entirely dead, away from the torments above. I sank down, surrounded by darkness. My head started to hurt. My heart strained. My chest felt crushed. I ignored it all. Soon, I stopped feeling the cold water around me. I felt nothing — except for a hand in mine.

When I opened my eyes again, I looked up at what appeared to be a cave ceiling. Blinking, confused, I glanced down at myself. Wrapped in furs, warm and snug, I wanted to lie my head back and enjoy the sensation, to fall back into my slumber. Then I jolted fully awake, remembering what had happened. Where was I? Sitting up slowly — my body ached to move — I saw the bed beneath me, a mattress made of feathers, a cotton cushion for my head.

Looking around, I saw that I was not in a cave but a small stone chamber. There were no windows or furniture save for the bed and a small stool. The air in the room felt muffled. Then I realised that I was actually surrounded by seawater. I could still breathe, but not as well. It wasn't unpleasant, but it meant I had to take deeper breaths. There was a door across the cobblestone floor, a great oak thing, slightly ajar. Then it was pushed further open.

A figure walked inside, female, tall, matronly, with long, dark, wavy hair. At first, I thought it was my mother, Rhea, but this woman had turquoise eyes and lines about her face. She was dressed in a floor-length navy gown, which glistened like the moon's light on the ocean's waves. Her shoulders were covered in a black silk shawl. She carried a silver tray in her elegant hands, on which lay clay bottles. She smiled when she saw me, as the door closed behind her of its own will. "It is good to see you awake, my lady. We were concerned you might sleep forever."

"We?" I muttered weakly.

"Okeanos and I," she said, sitting on the end of the bed, the tray on her lap.

I stared at her, my tired mind searching. "Tethys," I realised aloud.

She chuckled lightly. "Indeed, my lady."

"Was it you who saved me?"

She shook her head. "My husband."

I felt relief. "I thought it might have been my brother, Poseidon."

"When Okeanos returns, he will bring your presence to Poseidon's attention."

"Please, no. I would rather no one else know I am here."

"Why not, my lady?"

I hesitated, wondering if I should be honest. Still, etiquette dictated that I should give my hostess a reason for keeping my presence a secret. "I have run away."

"From Heaven, of all places?" Tethys raised an amused eyebrow. "You are the first, my lady."

"I cannot bear it anymore," I said, having no strength to explain.

She nodded. "Everyone has a limit."

Then I frowned. "How am I breathing at the moment? I am underwater."

"My husband's spell; the water will not drown you. However, you may feel a little light-headed from the lack of air."

Then she gestured to the bottles on the tray. "My lady, your body is under quite a bit of strain, not to mention the water pressure. So, I have provided an elixir to help you heal, nectar to build your strength, and a sleeping pharmakon to conserve your energy. I will bring you these every day for the next week. Once you are better, I shall feel no guilt letting you depart this place whenever you wish."

I took the bottles into my hands. "So, I am a prisoner?" I joked drily.

Tethys stood up. "Let yourself be mothered, my lady. Drink and sleep."

I swallowed the warm, sweet potions and fell back into the bed. For several days, but it felt like weeks, my aunt brought me nectar and ambrosia until I could sit in bed without pain.

Once I was strong enough to leave the chamber, Tethys guided me through her underwater home. The palace was like a great fortress on the outside, carved into the rock beds. Within the cavern was covered with coral reefs. The court of Okeanos and Tethys seemed to stretch on endlessly along the bottom of the ocean floor, lit only by the glimmering white light of those sea creatures who glowed of their own accord and whatever rays of Helios or light from Selene reached them through the depths.

The sea court was teeming with sea nymphs and fish of all breeds, colours, and sizes. Staring out of the windows, all was darkness in the deep sea around the palace, while inside, the sea court glimmered like a rainbow.

I met my host, Okeanos, a quiet sort, a god of muscle with scaly skin, dragon's wings, and a forked fishtail, often holding a huge harpoon for his sceptre. During my time there, he never revealed himself long enough to dine with his family or to speak with his wife. I could not help but notice the coldness with which he treated Tethys whenever they did happen to pass each other by. He granted me nothing more than a curt nod. At the same time, I heard from others how odd it was to see him at home, that he spent his days roaming the seas, his old kingdom, giving help to any who would accept it, primarily those who remembered the prehistoric days when he ruled the waves with a steady and fair hand. After the Titanomachy, he had willingly bowed on the battlefield to Poseidon, and relinquished power to him, promising him his fealty. However, according to Tethys, it seemed Okeanos had been lost since that day, trying to hold on to his former purpose with much difficulty and sorrow.

Tethys's children, the Okeanides, three thousand strong, also lived there. Once they overcame their wariness of me — for I was a sister of Poseidon, who had overthrown their father — they asked me stories about Heaven and listened with great curiosity. Although an outsider who did not belong, I was welcome. They stopped their staring. All but one.

Since the moment I had left the stone chamber where I had been nursed back to health, I had noticed from among the sea of strange faces and creatures a pair of sapphire eyes staring into mine. They were set in a pale, porcelain face with silver hair decorated in seashells that glinted a pearly pink in the watery moonlight. It was an unnerving feeling to be constantly watched like that. At length, I felt compelled to act.

"Who is she?" I asked Tethys one supper time as the nymph stared at me from further down the coral table. I nodded in her direction. "One of your daughters, I imagine?"

Tethys looked to where I was gazing. She cleared her throat. "Yes, my lady. Dione."

"Dione," I repeated in a whisper. "Do you know why she looks at me unrelentingly?"

Tethys pursed her lips, looking away. "I have my theories, but you must ask her yourself, my lady."

I determined to do just that — Tethys' response had made me even more curious. So, I went in search of Dione, following her pale figure through the underwater fortress, through its corridors. After she glanced at me over her shoulder, I realised that it was not so much me in pursuit but her in the lead.

At length, she stopped at the palace's gardens, where an enormous coral reef created an enclosure within which seaweed and water plants of every kind grew. At the sight of a princess of the deep and the Queen of Heaven, the other sea nymphs and creatures retreated into the shadows until it seemed to be just me and her alone together. I was not beguiled. It seemed to me that no one was ever on their own in this place. The water is a waiting, watchful witness and something in the depths is always listening.

Dione turned to face me. This Okeanid was even more beautiful up close. With fine features, silver locks, and wide sapphire eyes, she seemed ethereal. She was a true goddess of the sea dressed in robes made from dark green and red seaweed adorned with seashells. A string of pearls hung around her neck, black and milky white, and it glittered in the water. She bore a heavenly radiance I had not expected to see this far down in the deep, an enchanting glow as if from the moon. Everything about her seemed mysterious and secretive. *A fine contender for Aphrodite.*

"Dione, is it not?" I asked, refusing to be bewitched.

Her voice was silky. "Yes, my lady."

"I notice you keep looking my way. Is there a reason why I intrigue you so much?"

"Forgive me, my lady. I could not help it. For aeons, I have been wondering why he picked you," she replied, her sapphire eyes looking sorrowful as she floated towards me. "Now that you are here in the flesh, I see exactly why."

I frowned. "Him? Who are you talking about?"

"Zeus," she replied, as if it should be obvious. "My fiancé."

4: DIONE

"He never told you?" Dione asked, her eyes widening in realisation. Then she looked downcast. "I am not surprised. Why would he?"

"You were going to be Zeus's queen?" I swallowed hard, my throat tightening.

"That is what I once thought. In truth, I already believed myself to be his wife. In the days before the Titanomachy, before he slew Kronos and freed his siblings, he was mine alone," she explained, smiling sadly as she reminisced. "We would meet on the beaches, where the sea greets the sky. He would embrace me and talk of his dreams for the future, how he would overthrow the Titans and take his place as ruler of the cosmos, with me at his side. We were to divide the world between us and rule in harmony together."

My heart sank. If I had not known Zeus better, I could have sworn from her story that he had been in love with her.

She looked forlorn. "I believed him. And so, I gave him everything he wanted from me: my loyalty, my body, my heart. I even gave him a child."

I blinked. "What child?"

She did not seem to hear me, her lower lip quivering. "Perhaps that is why he left. What father desires a daughter?"

I tried to smile. "You gave him a daughter? How lovely."

"I thought so too. When I told him I was expecting, he seemed overjoyed. He swore to return to the shore to see his child in due course. I bore her in the sea foam. I did not think her sex would matter; he did not say it would. So I sent word to him that I had a daughter and that I had named her. I waited months and months on the coastline for him to come and claim her, but he never did. Maybe if it had been a son, he would have."

That sounded more like the Zeus I knew. "What happened to the child?"

She seemed to blush, looking at me with regret. "In my grief and hatred, not just at Zeus but at myself, I threw her into the waves and let her be washed away. Of course, I regretted it more than anything afterwards. I scoured the seas for her, the entirety of Okeanos's realm, even to the deepest point on the ocean floor where light does not live. When I gave up, I cursed myself for being the worst mother in the cosmos."

My heart grew heavy at her loss. "Had you given her a name?"

She smiled at the recollection as tears flowed down her face. "Yes, the one thing I did right by her: Aphrodite."

My stomach dropped. "Aphrodite?"

I recalled the day that the goddess of love had come into the throne room, how the whole world had been in awe of her, and how Zeus had been suspicious of her after she told him her name. It all made sense now — why he never pursued her. She was his daughter and my niece.

Dione smiled. "I know who she has become without me, and I am so proud of her. She believes herself to be the child of Ouranos, and I do not seek to ruin that fantasy. It is not my place to disturb her life when I refused to be her mother."

The sea nymph took my hands in hers. Her elegant fingers felt soft in the water. "My lady, I am glad I have told you this. I have been tormented for so long, afraid to show my face outside this palace, but now I see that the world does not even know my story in all this. So I can live for eternity in peace. However, please do not tell anyone, not even Aphrodite. I do not wish to uproot her life. All I ask of you, from one mother to another, is that you care for her in my absence. Keep her happy and safe as best you can. I am not there to be the mother she needs. Promise me."

I smiled reassuringly, overcoming my shock at her revelation. "I promise. In fact, she is to be married soon. But Aphrodite is a marvel to behold. She does not need mothering. She never did. There are some who doubt she even needs a husband."

Dione beamed, lifting her pale head up to look at the moonlight seeping in through the water. "That is good. Still, keep an eye on her, please. If she is anything like her father, she shall be difficult to reason with when challenged. However, if she is anything like me, she will be hurt easily should she make the wrong decisions. Guide her for me."

"She is my closest friend," I told her, sadly thinking back to my last conversation with the goddess of love. "There is nothing I would not do for her."

"Thank you, my lady."

As I turned back into the palace, my heart felt heavy. A past me might have shot from these depths to confront Zeus about his past with Dione. But I realised quickly as I stepped away that to bring the world's attention to Dione would not only endanger his authority but mine also.

Turning a corner, I bumped into my host Okeanos.

"My lord!" I gasped, stepping back. "Forgive me. My mind was elsewhere, and I did not watch my step.."

"The Queen of Heaven does not have to apologise to me," Okeanos grunted. He regarded me with a cautious, if slightly hostile, gaze.

Amid a suddenly awkward silence, I searched for something to say. "I wish to thank you for saving me. Your wife has been the most gracious hostess and nurse."

However, I realised, as I spoke, that Okeanos may have simply rescued me out of necessity, fearing the wrath of Poseidon, and not out of genuine kindness.

He did not seem interested in my gratitude. "As is expected of her."

I forced a smile. "She seems to be a wonderful wife, better than most. She is a caring mother to her children. She organises the court here. She arranges everything, apparently. You are blessed in her. You chose well."

"Yes, it seems I did." His tone was wary.

I could not help my curiosity. "Which is why I am confused."

He frowned, the scales on his face creasing. "Confused about what, my lady?"

"About why you do not speak to her. Has she offended you in some way?"

He scowled. "That is none of your concern, Hera. You are stepping outside the bounds of propriety for a guest."

"Queen Hera," I corrected him sharply, "and on the contrary. As the goddess of marriage, it is precisely my concern and my duty to enquire. It seems to me there is no fault with your wife which should cause you to ignore her, nor any fault with your family which would cause you to neglect them. So, the problem must be yours alone."

He gritted his sharp teeth. "Must it, my lady?"

I sighed. I did not wish to push him too far, for I had no allies at this court. Moreover, Tethys had not asked me to intervene. I chose my next words carefully. "Let me say this alone, and I beseech you to listen: you will never again be king under the sea," I told him gently. "However, you will always be a father and a husband. That purpose will always be with you. Speaking on behalf of wives, our entire existence is devoted to our husbands. When they do not return the care, it is an enormous pity and disappointment."

He clenched his jaw. Whatever he was thinking, he did not say it.

Moving around him, I went on my way. My heart was beating fast. Perhaps tough love had not been the best approach here, I wondered.

No, a voice said. *He's old enough to take it.*

From then on, the palace became tainted for me, that and the fact that the endless murky darkness and pressing currents disturbed me. I knew the time had come for me to depart. I had done my bit for Tethys's marriage in payment for her care. I could not tell whether my interference, albeit brief, had any effect. Still, I could not have left a married couple in turmoil without offering my aid somehow. It went against everything I stood for. At any rate, I did not have the strength nor the will to keep dispensing such advice. Eager to depart, I told my hostess I must move on with my journey, and a farewell ceremony from the whole Okeanid family was arranged.

I thanked my hosts before being escorted up through the ocean waves, black to blue, in a beautiful chariot made from a clamshell. It was decorated in mother-of-pearl, guided by a team of iridescent hippocampi, their elegant equine bodies heaving through the water as their fishtails powered me forward. However, my heavy eyelids were closed for most of the journey, as Tethys had given me a draught of sleeping pharmakon to ensure I was well-rested at the end of my journey, assuring me I would be placed somewhere far from Olympos so I could continue my exile in peace. Little did I know she took this so seriously that she sent me outside my husband's realm, beyond Hellas itself, to unknown lands.

5: SAMEIA

When I opened my eyes, I saw leaves dancing in the breeze above. A weeping willow tree towered over me, its drooping branches surrounding me as if I had been collected in its arms. Cool air tickled my skin. Then I heard the sound of lapping water. I sat up and saw that I was lying on the edge of a riverbank.

A god was before me, waist-deep in the water, his broad back to me. He had long brown hair, braided and interwoven with rushes. He was a dark figure against the shimmering water around him. He turned around and smiled at me with dimples dented into his cheeks. My throat ran dry as indigo eyes looked into mine.

"You are awake. At last." His voice was deep and smooth with a heavy eastern accent. The words rolled off his lips like water off a lily pad. He began to move towards me. "You have been asleep for many days. I was worried you might be as close to death as a goddess can get."

I swallowed the lump in my throat. "Who are you?"

He put a hand to his chest. "My name is Imbrasos. I am the god of this river."

"Where am I?"

"Far from home, closer to Anatolia than Hellas. This is the island of Samos." He spread his long arms as he waded closer. "I found you floating upstream on some driftwood. What is the last thing you remember?"

I did not need to think hard. "The sea," I replied.

"Yet you do not belong in the sea," he noted, raising an eyebrow. "What is the Queen of Olympos doing so far from her home and husband?"

I frowned. It unnerved me that he could tell who I was but I did not know him. "Is that your business?"

He shrugged. "I only saved your life and guarded you for several days, wondering what could have brought such a beautiful creature to these shores alone."

I struggled not to blush. "If my husband finds me here and learns you did not return me to Olympos, he shall persecute you."

Imbrasos grinned. "I would like to see him try."

I felt unbalanced at his response. If I had been standing, I might have fallen into the water. "You do not fear Zeus?"

He seemed unperturbed. "We are not in Hellas. Your husband's dominion does not stretch this far east. Zeus would be risking war with the gods of Anatolia if he were to come after me."

I blinked. "You mean that Zeus has no power in these parts?"

He shrugged. "He has power but no authority to use it. And so, you are safe here and most welcome for as long as you desire."

Briefly, I was comforted, but his words disturbed me. "How do you know I am in danger?"

His face darkened. "Reports from the Olympian court reach eastern shores frequently. We know of Zeus's wrath and of yours, too."

My face flushed. "I do not need your judgement."

"It is not judgement. It is, in a way, a question." He gave me a reassuring smile.

It took me a moment to understand his meaning and then I relaxed. He was giving me a chance to change the story known to him. His gaze was inviting, and I wanted to tell him but as I looked around, I felt it was not the right moment.

Beyond the willow tree's billowing leafy arms lay a green woodland, out from which poured the call of birdsong and rustling leaves, beckoning me to explore. With Imbrasos wading through the river, he showed me the nature of Samos. It was a beautiful place, one of the most radiant I had ever seen. It reminded me of the Garden of the Hesperides by Mount Atlas, with all kinds of trees and animals to behold.

The time I spent at Samos became one of the happiest times of my life. When the Samians realised I was there, they built a temple in my honour. I performed their marriage ceremonies for them, even tended to some births, and taught some young women, led by one called Admeta, a fiery maiden who had run away from home, a fellow Hellene. She, having been a priestess of mine previously, had gathered these women to teach them my ways and keep me company. They made sure I had all I needed, for I ensured they all found good husbands and delivered healthy babies. They showed me their ways too, making me a beautiful new dress, a tall headdress, adorning me in jewellery, and painting my skin.

My days were spent racing with the animals of the woods, riding the horses, and flying with the birds. I helped a golden gryphon bear her cubs, one of which, the runt of the litter, I fed myself. Being the weakest, he never grew wings and was little more than a lion with talons. So, I adopted him, and he went everywhere with me while his mother became my favourite way to fly around the island, and she was content to carry me. For this, my priestesses called me Hera Koutrophos, 'the nurturer'. I came across wild stallions, mares, peacocks, golden-horned cattle, multi-coloured snakes, hydras, and lions, all of whom provided me with further companionship. For this, the Samian women called me the Mistress of Animals. I soon found that I could tread anywhere and be greeted with friendliness. I felt like a completely different person, wilder, more powerful, and at peace. I could not call the island home just yet for my children were not here with me. But I wondered about bringing them to this place, away from the court and Zeus to a better existence.

Meanwhile, Imbrasos and I developed an affection for one another. I often joined him in the river, where he taught me to swim — I preferred the freshwater to the sea. We exchanged stories of our lives. I told him all I had done and seen and made him privy to my worst secrets, which he said he was honoured to know. I felt safe with him, for he was courteous and honourable, and there was nothing to fear from him. Every night, I took up my bed beneath that willow tree, and he would sometimes lie beside me, but never anything more.

The priestesses once jested that he was my husband as we sat in the woods. At first, I did not agree as we had not been joined in a ceremony and had not lain together. Furthermore, I reminded them, I had a husband back on Olympos.

"Does that truly matter, my lady?" Admeta asked, outspoken as ever which was always refreshing. "Is Imbrasos not kinder to you than Zeus ever was? Does he not act more like a husband should? Besides, who says one cannot have a spouse in one country and another elsewhere?"

I did not know how to answer that. Was such a thing possible? Was it even right?

As it turned out, I would not have to worry for long about what my connection with Imbrasos was becoming, for when Athena appeared, my idyllic interlude came to a swift end.

6: PLATAEA

I stood on the pale stony beach of Samos, looking out onto the vast open sea with shadows of islands on the horizon, their outlines visible on a clear day. It had been almost a year since I left Mount Olympos; time passed faster on Earth, so it was difficult to tell for sure. So far, I had no word from anyone, not even a whisper from a dryad of what was happening back home. Lately, the fog had been descending, a sign I had learnt which meant that Zeus was not as he should be, that something was wrong. Turning around and seeing Athena standing there in the sand, I knew I was right.

Dressed in full battle gear, her fair hair cut short, she looked fierce. Her silver eyes glinted in the light of Helios. She looked me up and down, one eyebrow arched, and commented: "You look different, my queen. Fatter, if I may."

I couldn't help but chuckle. She had always been impressive in both mind and manner. "Indeed. I have been well taken care of here. How have you been?"

She shrugged, glancing out to sea. "As ever, but the Olympian court is in turmoil. You have been gone so long that we wondered if you had been kidnapped. Zeus has sent out search parties all over the world. There were rumours that you were spotted in Euboea, so he made a trip there himself to find you. Of course, it came to nothing, and he was furious."

"He is concerned for me?" The idea confused me.

Athena frowned and hummed. "It is difficult to tell, but I think he recognises that his missing queen cannot be a good thing, if only because nothing is getting done. The staff in the palace are at a standstill with no direction. Mortal prayers on the mainland are going unanswered. The wedding of Hephaistos and Aphrodite has had to be postponed since you are not there to perform the ceremony."

A smile flickered over her mouth. "Pleased by your handiwork?"

I could not help but grin. "Only a little. I did not think my presence would be so missed."

"Well, you do not appear to have been kidnapped, so what am I to tell Zeus?"

I pursed my lips. "Be honest. Tell him that lying with Demeter was one step too far."

She hesitated. "He will not like that."

"I imagine not."

She stepped forward. "Hera, he will bring ruin down upon your head for such insolence."

"What do you imagine he has been doing to me so far?" I demanded.

She blushed. "I wish you would return with me. We can make up an excuse for your absence."

I shook my head. "I cannot live there, knowing he has lain with my sister. In all honesty, the move is overdue; I should have left long ago."

She nodded. "Then I will report as you wish. Once I do, you will receive other visitors, possibly even Zeus himself."

I sighed, not only saddened that my brief peace was coming to an end but also that my old life should collide with this precious haven. "I expect nothing less of him."

At dusk that evening, as I was roasting a rabbit over a fire, meditating on the sand and listening to the seagulls in the trees above, I heard footsteps behind me, a gait I knew by heart.

"What are you doing here?" I snapped, looking over my shoulder.

Demeter stood there. Her dark hair was done up in a braided bun at the back of her head. Over her white gown, she wore a ruby shawl around her shoulders, and her arms were lined with golden, bejewelled bracelets. She appeared more royal than she ever had before. I guessed it was because of Zeus's attentions, showering her with gifts he believed all females liked. They suited her, and that made my ichor bubble. However, her grey eyes were heavy with guilt and apprehension. In her strong arms, she carried a clay amphora.

"I could ask you the very same," she replied gently.

I rose to my feet, feeling the rage grow inside me. I thought of kicking her into the sea, of tearing her limbs apart, but I would not visit that horror upon the people of Samos. If peace was going to be disturbed here, it would not be by my hand. Instead, I looked around, searching for some inspiration. Then I gestured to my fire with the roasting spit. "Care to dine with me?"

She nodded, unsmiling. "Of course. As it happens, I brought mead."

And so, we sat in tense silence, munching on slightly burnt rabbit flesh, staring at the deep pink sunset in the misty sky. It was difficult to enjoy the taste of my dinner with Demeter sitting across from me. I tried to close my eyes and pretend she was not there. I tried to imagine anything else. Then my thoughts were interrupted.

"Hera," Demeter said, putting down a thigh bone. "You must know that I am here for more than just dinner. I expect that dining with me is one of the last things you desire right now."

I scoffed, bringing myself to look at her. "Not quite. It is the very last thing I desire. If Zeus were to bend me over this fire, taking me while my insides burned and I choked on the smoke, it would still hurt less than what you have done."

At first, she seemed taken aback. Then she blushed. "I deserved that, but I have a specific purpose: to ask you to return to Olympos with me."

I confess that I was astounded, if not impressed, by how she asked that of me. "If I would not oblige Athena, who has never done me any wrong, what in Chaos's great cosmos would make you think I would come with you?"

She fixed me with a determined gaze. "Because I know you better than Athena ever could. I know you better than Hestia or Aphrodite. I know you better than you probably realise."

I raised an eyebrow. "How do you figure that?"

"I am the closest to you in age and rank. I am more your equal than anyone else. So, I can understand your situation better than anyone else. That said, I know I have hurt you more than anyone else. For that, I will always be sorry. I let my desires ruin our sisterhood. While I could live with that regret, my existence would be unbearable to know that I was the reason you gave up what you love."

"You and Athena have more in common than you might imagine. She also presumed that I was content on Olympos," I snorted.

Demeter hesitated, glancing around. "This is a beautiful place, Hera. You have an eye for natural beauty, that is for sure. You deserve the freedom to see the world as you want without Zeus's permission. You are kind, caring, and selfless. You probably have many friends here already. This place would indeed satisfy much that you need."

She looked back at me. "Yet you are the goddess of family. You are meant to be with your kin, even if they cause you great pain, for they give you the great purpose of overcoming those challenges and creating an even stronger clan for it. You are meant to love others, Hera, especially those who do not deserve it, those like Zeus and me, because that is who you are. What would we do without you?"

I refused to take the bait. "You seem to have managed well without me so far."

She shook her head. "I am not well," she whispered, tears brimming her eyes. "I need your help."

She glanced down at her abdomen.

Immediately, I knew. *Got what you wanted then?* I thought viciously. "Go ask Eileithyia — childbirth is her dominion."

"She can only aid me when the day comes. You must help me now," she insisted.

I stood up, turning away. "I must do nothing. You do not deserve my help."

"Look at me," she begged, getting to her feet. "Please."

I felt her hand on my wrist and yanked myself away from her. "Do not touch me."

"I did not enjoy it, you know," she whispered after a moment's hesitation.

I closed my eyes. "You sought him out."

"He sought me out."

"Yet you did not refuse him."

"Neither did you."

I whirled around to face her. "I did refuse him!"

"Yet you became his all the same," she continued, sighing in exasperation. "Zeus gets what he wants, one way or another. It would not have made any difference if I had refused him. I would still be here today begging for your help."

I took a deep breath as my eyes stung. "It is not the fact that you lay with him which hurts, but the fact that you did it so willingly, so readily."

"Would you have preferred it if I had been unwilling?" Her voice was quiet.

I could not answer that.

Demeter huffed. "All I wanted was another chance to be a mother, a good mother. Zeus gave me that chance, despite what it meant and I thought any sacrifice would be worth it. But I now realise that it wasn't. I do not wish to raise my child in a world where the goddess of motherhood has turned her back on me, my own sister. My baby sister."

The tears burst through me, and I had to look away from her as I sobbed. Grief and rage mixed in my mind, and I hoped she would turn away and leave me. But she did not. I felt a tender hand on mine and she held my palm to her lower abdomen.

"Tell me what you feel."

Once she did that, I could not resist. I felt the light of life inside her, its warm glow, and then I knew, deep down, that I would worry for her and her baby. I would not be able to help myself.

"It is healthy," I whispered, looking back at her through a blurred vision. I took my hand back and wiped my eyes.

A beam of delight spread across her face, and a tear trickled down her cheek. Then she embraced me. Her arms were warm and soft. "Thank you, Hera. Thank you so much."

At first I was tense and unwilling. But she did not retract. She smelled of home, and it had been so long since I had been lovingly embraced by one of my own. Before I could command myself otherwise, my arms were around her. Soon, I found myself weeping into her shoulder.

What other option was there?

She parted from me and kissed me softly on the forehead. Then she grew serious. "If you do not come back with me tonight, the next face you see shall be your husband's, and it may very well be the last thing you ever see."

A shiver ran down my spine, but I remained steadfast, remembering Imbrasos's assurance that Zeus had no authority here. "His was also the first I ever saw. What a poetic ending that would be."

Demeter smiled sadly. "As you wish. I must go now."

When I opened my eyes the following day, as they became accustomed to the sunlight shining from above, I also saw something else: my husband over me, the sun behind his head and his figure dark, but I recognised him all the same. Panic seized my heart. Getting to my feet, the wind blowing away my slumber, I stood before him.

Dressed in his royal raiment, with a crown upon his head, there was no doubt he wished to let all the barbarians of Samos know his status. He was holding my queenly garments in his arms: a white embroidered gown, a golden diadem, and the golden sandals he gave me for our wedding. He regarded me with a calm expression, but I expected he was bubbling underneath.

"My lord," I muttered, curtseying. My heart was beating frantically inside my chest.

I glanced at the nearby river flowing alongside us. Imbrasos was nowhere to be seen. I breathed a small sigh of relief. The last thing I needed was for Zeus and him to meet.

"Here," he said, pushing the word through his teeth. "I thought you might want these. Living in the wilderness can be a dirty business. Fresh clothes will make you feel better."

The dutiful wife in me overtook momentarily, and I took them. "Thank you."

"Hebe is wondering when you are coming home. For that matter, so am I," he said, his words clipped.

"I do not know," I said in a hoarse voice.

"Surely, you have a date in mind? You do not plan on abandoning your duties forever, do you? Your children need you. Your husband needs you."

I could not help but snap back: "Does he truly?"

His haughty exterior flickered. "What do you mean?"

For a moment, I hesitated. Was it worth it? I decided that it was. It was high time.

I took a deep breath. "When you lay with the mortal women, the Titanesses, and the nymphs, I could think that maybe, just maybe, I was still important enough to you. Now, you have bedded an Olympian, our sister, not to mention my elder." My voice broke, though I tried not to lose myself entirely. "A wife cannot control her husband's desires. I accept that. Yet it would be nice if, just once, he considered hers."

He raised an eyebrow. "Very well, what do you desire?"

His question, so inconsiderate as if he had never wondered it before, felt like a slap across the face. Did he have no empathy? "I would have preferred for you to not bed my sister," I spat.

"Do you want me to say I will never desire Demeter again?" He bared his teeth. "What right do you have to ask that of me?"

I clenched my jaw. *What arrogance!* "A right that my husband be faithful. A right that, at the very least, my children be the highest of Olympians after you. A right that my own throne is secure!" I exclaimed in frustration, dropping his gifts on the ground, letting my diadem clatter over the rocks and my clothing fall in disarray.

Zeus leaned forward, hissing. "How dare you? You get everything you want."

Heart racing, my mind thought fast, and words came to me swiftly: "Except you!"

He faltered. "What?"

"You give your attention to all but me. Do you deny that?" I asked him, putting on a beggar's tone.

I fell to my knees before him. The words came tumbling out of my mouth easier than I had anticipated. I could not tell whether they were lies or not. Tears started flowing from my eyes, and I was unsure if they were real. "All I want is your devotion, my lord. It is all any wife desires. Rarely do I get it, and I am supposed to be the goddess of marriage, your queen! We are meant to be the example."

He was silent for a moment and then: "Hera, you, above all others, have my devotion. Have I ever left you on the wayside? Have I ever turned my back on you?"

What rubbish. I spluttered. "Each time you climb into another's arms, no matter who they are, my heart breaks. I withstand it as best I can. It is what all wives must endure. But Demeter? That is too much for me to bear."

I placed my wet face in my palms, exhausted. I had said my piece, and I accepted whatever would happen next.

To my confusion and surprise, I felt Zeus's arms around me. He hushed me softly as he pulled me to my feet.

"Hera, you must see sense. You are the queen, the highest of goddesses. Your children are the most important in the court. I did not think you would need to be told that. Besides, what god spends his time talking with his wife, especially a king? I have more important things to do in the day."

I kept my gaze on the ground. I was worried that if I looked him in the eye, he would see some lie that I sensed but could not find, for I knew I was speaking some truth. "You have all the time in the world and none for me. Show me that I am not just another of your concubines."

He huffed and let go of me. "Very well. Come home, and I will do just that. But I expect you by nightfall. Only then will I give you any special attention, Hera, not that you deserve it. A wife has her duty to her husband first before his to her."

With that, Zeus turned, charged down the beach, and stormed into the sky, lightning flashing all around, leaving me in the middle of my madness.

Perhaps he had expected me to follow him. Maybe I would have obeyed if he had not ended our quarrel in that manner, with those words. Yet he did, and so I did not.

The following day, Athena arrived early. Skipping the pleasantries, she came straight to the point. "Zeus wants the diadem he brought you yesterday."

"Why?"

She hesitated, swallowing. "He is getting married today."

I felt winded, too shocked to speak.

A pained look came over her face. "Someone called Plataea, a daughter of Asopos, whoever he is."

"A wedding?" I breathed.

"Yes. Apparently, she is to be our new queen on Olympos."

Our new queen. At first, I was shocked. Perhaps I should have realised this might indeed happen, that Zeus would replace me, but, for some reason, I did not. Maybe I thought that after the way he dismissed Thetis, such a thing would never happen.

Dione's face flashed across my mind, and the injustice settled in. I would not let myself be cast aside so quickly as she had been, wallowing in self-pity as an exile, afraid to even show my face because of the humiliation that I was not enough. I clenched my jaw. I was his queen. He had made me thus, against my own wishes, without my permission. I could not let all my struggles since then be for nothing.

I turned my face to the sky and scowled. *Let the Moirai pour over their precious string as they will,* I thought. *I shall have my marriage and be happy in it.*

It was the last reaction I thought I would have: to fight for my position as Zeus's wife. Yet, without a second thought, I donned my dress, sandals, and diadem. Upon calling out for my Samian golden gryphon, which roared out in response, the strength of her wings on the wind shook the crowns of the trees before landing on the ground before me, sending tremors into the earth and dirt up into the air. I mounted her with a stunned Athena by my side and flew to my husband's wedding.

It was being held in a temple dedicated to me, of all jokes and insults. After dismounting the gryphon, which let out a mighty roar to let all know I had arrived — the best type of fanfare I can assure you — I stormed up the steps and through the double doors with Athena hot on my tail, asking me with uncertainty in her voice what I was planning.

Before me, the aisle was lined with courtiers and, at the far end, my family, who were willing to witness this atrocity with no objection on my behalf. Zeus stood before the altar with a woman by his side. She was dressed in white, with a diadem, just like mine, on her head.

"Zeus!" I roared.

The augur stopped preaching.

All heads turned towards me. Complete silence.

"You want a queen? Well, here I am!" I yelled, my words ringing out.

Murmurs erupted around the temple.

Zeus turned to face me. He seemed momentarily shocked but quickly recovered, his silver eyes flashing with annoyance as I charged down the aisle towards him and his bride.

He declared loudly for the congregation to hear: "Hera, you have refused to behave as a wife and mother should. I need a queen I can rely upon. Do not blame me for having to make do without you. You missed your chance to salvage this marriage."

Ignoring him, I focused on his bride-to-be, who had her back to me. "Plataea, is it? I have never heard the name before," I snapped.

"Her father is a river god from Anatolia," Zeus informed me from the side.

"Anatolia?" I repeated, laughter bursting from my chest. "She is not even Hellenic!"

"Hera, control your temper," he hissed. "Stop making a spectacle of yourself."

"I have been controlling my temper for long enough!" I fumed at him. "Face me, you wretch!" I ordered Plataea.

Still, she kept her back to me.

I put my hand on her shoulder. "Look at me when I speak to you!"

Upon grabbing her dress and whirling her around, she turned with unexpected ease as if she barely weighed more than a branch. With the force of my grip, I completely tore the fabric off her body. Yet all that stood underneath was a thin body of wood. Her face was made of wood. No features. No mouth. No eyes. Nothing. All that stared back at me from under a veil was a simple plank.

Shocked, I stepped back and glanced between the plank bride and my husband. "You are marrying a tree?" I asked, bewildered.

Zeus burst into laughter. "No, Hera!" He removed the veil and quickly picked up his bride, throwing her to the ground. "She is not real!"

I stared down at the lifeless, unmoving statue. "What?"

He spread his arms and gestured to the temple. "This is all a sham! A trick."

Blinking, I looked around and saw the smiles on everyone's faces. Humour. Kindness. Relief. Delight. Excitement.

"I do not understand," I breathed, turning back to him.

Zeus approached and took my face in his hands. "I gathered them all here today so they can see my true queen, the only one I will ever have at my side." He kissed me softly on the lips. "You."

For a very brief moment, it was as if all my wishes had come true, the dream realised, that Zeus was capable of being all I had hoped for. It was the closest I ever came to loving him. But the feeling was gone almost as soon as it had been born.

The world around us erupted in cheers. The augur declared that we had renewed our vows. Zeus turned and led me out of the temple to a ready chariot. The spectators came after. He smiled and waved at them, without looking at me save to plant a final kiss on my cheek as we departed for Olympos.

7: KORE

When Demeter went into labour, Olympos had a buzz of anticipation. The courtiers were constantly in the throne room asking Zeus questions about it, which he seemed more than happy to answer. He ensured she received the appropriate care and attention from all the physicians and midwives, something he had never bothered to do for me. However, I had never required such help.

Nymphs had been coming in and out of my chambers since news of Demeter's labour had started, telling me how it was going. It grew tedious. I ordered them to only return with information of what sex it was: if male, Demeter would be venerated. Finally, the nymphs returned at dusk to tell me that a baby girl named Persephone was born to the world. A small wave of relief came over me. Yet when I was asked if I wished to skip the queue outside her quarters to see the newly born baby, there was no hesitation in my refusal. No, I would see enough of both her and the child for the rest of time. Although, I could not help feeling a twinge of jealousy. At no point during the myriad of births I had undergone had courtiers lined up outside my bedchamber, waiting impatiently to see any of my newly born children.

Demeter suckled Persephone herself, refusing wet nurses; she declined the help of handmaidens and even withstood Zeus's encouragements to put his new daughter in the Olympian nursery and have me rear her. Demeter seemed utterly devoted to her new child and insisted on doing everything herself.

Decreed to be the goddess of plant life, Persephone was gorgeous, and everyone doted on her. Sweet and polite, she became the court's darling. Surprisingly, she had not been born with her father's golden hair like most of his other children. Instead, she had long ebony locks and Zeus's silver eyes.

At first, I could not understand the fuss, although I suspected I would have never seen her the same way as others. Still, I stayed away from Demeter and her daughter unless out of necessity, even though I recognised that Persephone had not harmed me.

In the meantime, I had little contact with Zeus. The charade he had arranged at the fake wedding to Plataea, the joy he had displayed at being reunited with his actual wife and queen, had since evaporated. Things were as bad as ever, if not worse. Zeus had demanded I release my gryphon and her offspring, including the wingless lion I had adopted, as well as an infant hydra, all of which I had brought back from Samos. With a heavy heart, I let them off into the wild. Zeus allowed me to keep my peacocks to pull my chariot because they were not threatening beasts and were beautiful to behold, a spectacle for the courtiers. Amid disappointment in him, I focused on Hebe, who was nearing maidenhood.

One day, there was an unexpected knock on my bedchamber door. When I opened it, I saw Persephone standing there with her large eyes twinkling up at me. She had grown so quickly. She curtseyed poorly. "Sorry, miss Hera, have you seen Mama?"

My heart warmed and I said, "No, but you can wait in here until she comes and finds you."

I opened the door further and gestured inside where there were plenty of playthings and Hebe for company. She nodded shyly, accepted my invitation, and came inside. Now, you may wonder if this was when I thought to harm my husband's bastard daughter. If so, banish those thoughts from your mind — I could never have hurt my sister's child, despite what Demeter had done to me. I found Persephone to be quite a lively girl. She chatted happily about the plants of the gardens and the woods outside. I watched, played with, and fed her until her mother came to fetch her.

It was not long before Persephone wormed her way into my heart, knocking on the door of my bedchambers to deliver flowers she had picked or always greeting me with an enthusiastic smile and excited wave whenever I passed her by. I cared for her when Demeter could not. I told her stories of the Titanomachy and how Zeus came to rule the world. I told her about what marriage prospects lay before her. Unlike her mother, she seemed to enjoy the idea, which was pleasantly surprising. In time, I grew to love her. She reminded me of the childhood innocence that Demeter and I had once possessed in our first days in this world. Her naivety stayed with her even when, not long after, she reached maidenhood, by which time she was affectionately known as Kore, and had become a beautiful princess.

It was early in the evening, walking through the palace gardens, when I stumbled across Kore huddled underneath a tree, her legs bent up to her face, her eyes closed, whimpering. Her long dark hair was a dishevelled mess.

I kneeled beside my niece and touched her arm gently. "Kore, what is wrong?"

Looking up, she saw me. Her eyes were filled with tears.

"Oh, my queen. I am sorry you have seen me like this!" she sobbed.

Settling beside her, I waited patiently for her to calm down so she could tell me, although I dreaded what she would say.

"What are you doing out here alone? It is almost nightfall. You should be inside."

"Forgive me, my lady," she sniffled. "I did not want to go inside while he was there."

I frowned. "Who? Has someone scared or threatened you?"

She nodded, face crumpling. "Yes. Hermes," she replied, voice breaking.

I drew back, alarmed. "What has he done? Did he harm you?"

Her lower lip wobbled. "He tried to, my lady."

"Yet he did not succeed?"

She shook her head. "No, my lady. Mother told me to scream whenever someone touched me. I did not want to, but I did, and he ran away."

I raised an eyebrow. "You gave him a fright, then?"

"This time, my lady. Yet I fear he may try again."

I put my arms around her. "That will not happen. Let us go inside, find your mother, and tell her. She will make sure you are always escorted. Hermes would not dare approach with a chaperone present. He only tried this time because you were alone."

We walked back to the palace through the woods in the moonlight and headed for my bedchamber. Once Kore was safely inside, I went to fetch my sister.

Deep down, I was stunned. *Who would have thought Hermes capable of such a thing?* Yes, he was a scoundrel at the best of times. Still, he had never before, to my knowledge, resorted to completely disregarding the feelings of others and causing them such pain.

At my beckoning, Demeter swiftly returned to my quarters with me. There, she comforted her daughter and cursed Hermes, swearing he would learn his lesson. The following day, she must have told Zeus what had happened because my husband angrily summoned Hermes to a private audience. When he did not show, Zeus rampaged through the city in search of him. Perhaps, against all others, Hermes would have succeeded in his attempt to escape, but Zeus was too clever and powerful. He tracked Hermes down and dragged him through the palace, in front of all, to the throne room. Courtiers poured in, curious to see what was going on. Gods watched from their thrones.

Releasing his hold, Zeus threw Hermes to the floor. Angry lightning flashed behind his eyes. After regaining his composure, Hermes stood straight, facing his father, patting down his dishevelled, fiery red hair. He met his father with boldness, as Zeus circled him like a lion his prey.

"I had wished to do this more discreetly, but your insolence calls for public attention," Zeus growled. "Your tricks have gone too far. You assault my daughter, Kore, then disobey your king's command to answer for your behaviour."

The King of Olympos ceased pacing. "The wiles of females often intoxicate, but there is little excuse for a god to lose his reason. You must control your lust. However, disobeying me? That is another offence entirely."

"Fear of your power caused me to flee, my lord," his son said, keeping his gaze low. "Please accept my humble apologies. It shall not happen again."

I rolled my eyes and glanced over at Demeter, where I saw a fire behind her eyes. On the other hand, Kore blushed and kept her eyes down. I knew that she wished to be anywhere else.

Zeus sat down on his throne. "And your apology for your offence against Kore?"

Hermes lifted his chin in defiance. "My lord, I committed no crime against her."

Zeus scowled. "You attempted to take her honour."

Hermes flushed. "I failed. Is failure a crime, my lord?"

I had to bite the inside of my cheek to not scoff. My fingers flexed, wishing to strike him down.

Zeus pursed his lips, tapping the arm of his chair. "No, but you meant to succeed."

Hermes huffed. "I am sorry if I scared her."

Zeus shook his head. "You do not seem to understand the consequences of what might have happened. Kore is an Olympian princess — my daughter. If you had besmirched her reputation, what would have become of her? It would have reflected badly on the entire family, including you."

He glanced over to his daughter. "Yet I hear she took matters into her own hands to make sure that did not happen. So it seems I have a wise daughter but a fool for a son!"

"I have apologised, my lord, for both offences."

Zeus stood up from his throne. "Yes, you have. To be clear, should you risk the reputation of anyone in our family, Hermes, you will find yourself without any family at all, or worse."

The trickster god nodded.

"You are dismissed," Zeus decreed.

With that, Hermes stormed from the room, glaring at Kore.

After word spread of Hermes's overzealous hands, other bachelors of the court tried to win Kore. However, none would have her hand, Demeter swore. None was good enough. However, despite what she wanted, the Moirai had other plans.

I had been fast asleep when Demeter, fully dressed, burst into my room a few nights later, slamming the door against the wall. I bolted upright in bed, blinking madly at the sudden light entering my dark room. I rubbed my eyes, seeing Demeter. Before I could say anything, she threw herself at me.

"Kore is gone. You must help me."

"What?"

"Help me, Hera. My daughter is missing!"

Her words sank in. "What do you mean? When did you last see her?"

"In the woods this evening. She was picking flowers for me. She has not come back. I went out there myself but I could not find her."

I hastily rose from my bed. "We must raise the alarm."

Soon everyone in Olympos was awake and gathered in the great hall, where Demeter was shouting instructions to search every nook and cranny of the palace. Everyone was eager to help instead of returning to their beds. Kore had been the light and life of the court for many years. Her absence was a calamity. The scene was chaotic, with courtiers and nymphs dashing about the place, running into each other and reporting to Demeter that the princess was nowhere to be found, as my sister became more distressed.

Finally, Zeus arrived. He entered the throne room, his golden hair a tousled mess and the beginnings of a short beard on his chin. He rubbed his eyes as he entered, his grey gaze angered with the interruption of the clamouring courtiers.

Everyone fell still and silent at his approach.

Demeter rushed up to him. "Kore is missing."

He frowned, not sharing her hysteria. "Where was she last?"

"The woods! She never came back," Demeter cried. "What will we do?"

He clenched his jaw, thinking. Then he said: "Where is Hermes?"

Demeter gasped in shock. "You think he is responsible?"

Zeus moved past her, staying silent.

She stared after him in horror, her eyes shining.

I rushed to her side, wrapping my arm around her in support.

Zeus climbed the dais and sat on his throne. "Where is Hermes? Fetch him here."

After much scouring from all, Hermes was brought before the king. "What now?" he grumbled, still rubbing his eyes after being dragged out of bed.

"You can redeem yourself after your assault on Kore."

Hermes huffed. "How so?"

Zeus gestured for him to come closer, right up to his face. Then the king leaned forward and whispered something so faint into his son's ear that even those closest could not discern what was said. Hermes muttered something in reply. His father shook his head, straightened up, and said: "Find her. Bring her safely home. Then you shall be redeemed."

Hermes bolted from the room, pushing past anyone standing in his way.

Demeter stepped forward, addressing the king. "Where is he going? Where is Kore?"

Zeus got up from his throne. "I do not know for certain, sister. Otherwise, I would fetch her myself, but I have sent Hermes, who will not return until he knows her whereabouts."

He started to walk back down the room towards the double doors, his footsteps resounding on the marble floor. "Now, I am retiring. I suggest you all do the same. We shall discuss this in the morning. Goodnight, all."

After the king's departure, chatter broke out among the courtiers. They left for their rooms, leaving just Demeter and me behind.

"Hermes will find her," I reasoned. "He will not rest until he does."

"Nor will I," she snapped, turning to face me. "Do you think I would leave my daughter's rescue to Hermes, of all entities? He has never taken anything seriously. He has recently proven that he cares nothing for my daughter's welfare. I am her mother. I cannot sit by or put my trust in the competency of others. So, I will go, too, and I shall not return until I have her safely in my arms."

"I shall come with you." The words were out of my mouth before I could stop them.

Demeter smiled gratefully. "Hera, no. Thank you, but you are needed here. Zeus would not allow it after you left for so long last time."

I pursed my lips. She was right, yet my care for Kore was more substantial than any consideration for Zeus. I was adamant about accompanying her. "I, too, cannot sit here wondering about her fate and yours. It would be too much."

She blushed. "I do not deserve your help after what I did."

"You are my family, Demeter. So is Kore. I do not know if you have heard: there is nothing more important to me than family," I reassured her, realising at that moment that I had forgiven her sin against me without any penalty.

Demeter smiled, her eyes shining. "Thank you."

We might have embraced tightly if there had been the time, but there was not. We departed Olympos straight away.

8: ERINYS

For nine days, Demeter and I roamed Hellas in search of Kore. Dressed as old women so we would pass largely unnoticed and uncared for, we scoured the land together.

Whilst searching for Kore, Demeter could not tend to her duties as goddess of the harvest, so the crops of Hellas began to fail in the searing heat. Fresh grain wilted. Fruit and vegetables withered. With supplies low and nothing suitable for harvesting, many began to starve. First, the elderly, the very young and the sick, but soon even the strong began to grow weak. Beggars grabbed at our cloaks and pleaded for the food we did not have. It was distressing to see the poor dying on roadsides and in the gutters of the cities we travelled through.

We began by wandering through the lands of Attica. As we proceeded on our journey, Demeter showed little tolerance for those who offended her and blessed those who showed humility, manners and help. When night fell, we huddled together under a tree for shelter from the rain or, if a house was nearby, we knocked on the door and were often granted sanctuary. Hospitality was a crucial Hellenic custom.

One evening, as dusk was almost settled, we were hobbling along an uneven country road. In the distance, we saw a low torchlight and determined to reach it before we had to sleep in the shrubbery again. And soon enough, after we walked down a few more pathways, we came to a rustic stone dwelling. It seemed strong enough to keep out the cold wind and the pouring rain. So, we approached, and Demeter rapped her knuckles upon the door. When there was no reply, she knocked louder for a second time.

Her call was answered by a woman already in her nightdress with a woollen shawl wrapped around her shoulders, her long dark hair reaching down her back. She was not old. Her complexion was healthy, and her countenance did not bear any humility at the sight of two old women. Instead, it was more like a foul odour had disturbed her peace.

"Dear lady," Demeter croaked, hunching over to exaggerate her humpback. "You have nothing to fear from us. May we please take shelter in your home tonight? We are just old women with no family near to whom we can go. So, it is to you we must appeal or face the harsh elements of the night."

The lady pursed her lips, not seeming too moved by Demeter's supplications. "My husband is not home. Such decisions are usually made by him," she said in a clipped tone. "But I suppose he would be angered if he discovered I had turned away strangers in need, especially elderly women such as yourselves. Come in."

She slowly pulled the door open.

"Thank you, dear lady," Demeter cawed, pushing her way past the woman.

"Please, call me Misme," our host replied, smiling curtly.

Silently, I followed my older sister inside.

The small house was warm and dry, with candles burning softly. Going into the front room, Demeter grabbed a stool and gestured for me to sit down, so I obliged her.

Misme appeared in the doorway. "Do you have anything for safekeeping?"

"No, thank you," Demeter replied. "However, we would not mind some water and food."

"Of course," Misme said and moved out of sight into the back of the house.

I gave Demeter a sideways glance. She bore a twinkle of amusement in her eye.

Misme returned quickly with a basket of fruit and cold-cooked meats, which she placed on a table in front of us. "This is all the food I have to spare."

Demeter examined the platter and made a dissatisfied grunt.

Misme's pleasant countenance faltered. "The harvest has not been good this year. Many suffer the same. I hope you understand."

Demeter looked her up and down. "Stop squirming like you are trying to hold in a stool, woman. This will do just fine."

Misme's eyes widened at my sister's rudeness, but she just nodded. Even women in her position, whose authority lay within the home, had to respect their elders.

A giggle sounded from behind our host.

I peered around Misme to see a boy hovering in the doorway, no older than ten years, with dark brown hair and a rosy glow in his cheeks, dressed in a short tunic and barefoot, possibly having arisen from bed to see what visitors had come into his father's house. He peeked at us from behind his mother, curious about the two old crones.

I smiled. "Who is this young gentleman?"

"This is Askalabos, my only son." Misme smiled. She beckoned him. "Greet our guests. Pour them a drink."

Askalabos bowed his head before entering. He handed me a cup of water poured from the amphora. "Here, madam," he muttered shyly.

"Thank you, dear," I said, taking it from him. Examining the cup, I saw that within the water floated pennyroyal and barley oats. I gladly took a sip.

He gave Demeter a cup, and she eagerly glugged down the contents, slurping loudly as the liquid drooled down her chin and dripped onto her lap.

Relatively few times had I seen Demeter drink so messily, so I stared at her. She must have been thirsty, or perhaps it was part of the act. I could not tell.

A little giggle came from the boy, Askalabos, as he watched her.

I glanced at his mother, who did nothing to check her child's conduct, and frowned.

Demeter stopped drinking and looked at the boy. "What is so funny, young master?"

He ceased laughing and looked up at his mother for permission to speak.

Misme scoffed. "Oh, just the way you were drinking, my lady."

"Excuse me?"

Then Askalabos giggled: "Do you need a deeper jar?"

Demeter blinked. Then, striking out her hand, she threw the rest of the water in his face. She lunged forwards, grabbed the amphora from his arms, and emptied what was left over his head, dousing him until he was soaked through.

I jumped up from my seat in shock.

Crying out, Askalabos looked down at himself in surprise and then up at the enormous old hag. He backed up, eyes filling with tears.

Misme stared at Demeter in horror. "How dare you! That is against the rules of hospitality, you know — attacking your host."

Demeter wore a wicked grin. "Is that so? Well, so is laughing at your guest." Then she clicked her fingers.

Askalabos cried out in pain, doubling over.

Misme turned to her son's aid. "Askalabos? My treasure, what is it?"

Already Demeter's curse was taking hold. The boy's fingers were turning green. As he turned his head upwards, he no longer wore the face of a boy but a diamond-shaped head with large bulging eyes on the sides. When he opened his mouth to cry for help, all that came out was a forked tongue and a croak of alarm. A long, scaled tail, green like olives, had already grown out of his behind. His skin shed, revealing a thick coat of bumpy multicoloured bumps. He fell forward on all fours, his hands and feet transforming into large green claws. Then, he shrunk to no more than the size of his mother's foot. His cries turned into strangled calls as Askalabos had become a gecko. Whether or not Askalabos could now understand his new situation, he scurried around, bumping into his mother's feet.

Misme stared at her son in horror. "What have you done to my boy?" she wailed. She picked him up, cradling him in her arms. "Askalabos! Can you hear me?"

"He cannot understand you," I said gently.

Demeter discarded her cloak, revealing who she really was. "Such is the price for disrespect."

I stood up, too, taking off my hood.

Misme gazed at us. "Oh, my," she muttered, falling to her knees. Tears were in her eyes as she looked up at us, trapped between wonder and grief.

"This is why hospitality is valued — you never know who a guest may truly be," I told her.

Demeter turned to me. "Sister, we shall find nothing but dishonour in this place. We shall take our leave now." She looked down on Misme. "No doubt, when your husband returns, you shall have to explain why his only son is an amphibian." My sister picked her cloak off the ground and started to move past the woman, beckoning me to follow.

"W-what will I say?" Misme stammered, calling after us.

"The truth. Say that you failed as a mother by not teaching him manners," she told her.

With that, we left, disappearing into the night; sleeping on the curb was more comfortable than dealing with rude mortals.

Demeter's humour was no better in Argolis, where a certain Kolontas refused to let us stay in his house one night. His daughter, Chthonia, disapproved and let Demeter inside. My sister, after revealing herself, ordered Chthonia to travel to Hermione and build a temple there for her. Chthonia eagerly obeyed, content to leave her ungodly father. Then, Demeter burned down his house, and he burned too.

We scoured the coastline of Hellas. We visited various islands, one of which belonged to Apollo. The sirens, daughters of the river Achelous and the Muse Melpomene, refused to help us. They were turned into flying demons, a cross between bats and eels, forever cursed to sing for help to passing sailors, who, enchanted by the sound, would quickly abandon their ships to swim to them, either drowning or being dashed on the treacherous rocks where the sirens lived.

Then we ventured north to Thessaly, where we found King Erysichthon, a large man dressed in much finely dyed fabric and jewellery of his station. He had ordered his slaves to cut down a grove sacred to my sister to make way for an extension of his palace. Upon doing so, they found one tree where votives to her had been made, so his slaves refused to fell the tree. After snatching an axe from a slave, Erysichthon began hacking at it mercilessly, a manic fury in his eyes.

Demeter and I watched the scene from among the thick brambles.

Almost immediately, the tree's green foliage turned black with rot. The long branches of the crown drooped, casting a dark pall over the king. The dead leaves and acorns were too weak to hold on to the branches and tumbled to the ground, where the tree roots were already rotting. Erysichthon chopped at the trunk, but the wooden shards did not fly out as expected. Instead, deep red blood seeped down from the wound, bleeding like from a slaughtered bull on an altar. He did not seem to notice, pillaging the trunk.

The slaves gasped in shock, pointing at the dying tree. One of them surged forward. "Master, do not!"

The king shoved him to the ground with one push of his hand. "Back off, fool that you are for praising mere trees!"

He raised the axe high and, in one fell swoop, cleaved the trunk in half.

Blood burst from it like a geyser.

A voice came from the tree's heart: "Being a nymph of this tree, I was loved by Demeter. So, I can die happy. But you, Erysichthon, shall be punished for this sacrilegious crime."

I shuddered to listen to the dying words of the dryad while Demeter sucked in a breath, tears streaming down her cheeks.

Erysichthon dropped his axe, shocked to hear the voice, realising what he had done.

The fallen slave scrambled to his feet and, with his companions, hurried away, not wanting to be part of the curse which would soon follow.

Demeter wiped her face and pushed through the bushes, appearing before him.

Erysichthon fell to his knees, awed and afraid, trembling and sweating.

My sister snapped at him in her fury: "Erysichthon of Thessaly, for your hubris, for denying your people this grove from which they could eat, and for destroying my tree where I received worship, you shall starve, and no amount of my food shall ever satisfy you."

After Demeter spoke, she turned away, leaving the curse to take hold and letting the sister dryads of the grove come forth to mourn the passing of their fellow nymph. She called upon an Oread, a mountain nymph, to visit the goddess Famine, whom Demeter was never to meet directly, and command her to never let grain grow in Thessaly nor to let food satisfy the king's stomach.

Erysichthon grew very large in his quest to satisfy his hunger. He even sold his daughter into slavery for more food. As she was loved by Poseidon, the god allowed her to transform into different creatures, so she escaped effortlessly, but when Erysichthon realised this, he kept repeatedly selling her to buy food. Still, he could not fend off starvation and finally ate himself instead.

Throughout our journey, I supported Demeter, tolerating her whims and moods. I did not question her actions: anger and fear are not natural bedfellows of mercy or generosity. However, by the seventh day, her determination had started to dwindle. Her mood began to lower. Her resolve was disappearing. That afternoon, we had already been wandering through the woods for some time, trying to find shelter in the undergrowth before dusk dropped on the mortal world, when Demeter raised her hand, halted, and exclaimed. "There! Do you see?"

I looked at where she was pointing. Peering through the trees, I saw a small cavern on the mountainside.

She shrugged. "As good a place as any. Let us sleep there for the night."

And so, I followed her to shelter from the wind and rain.

We lit a small fire, and Demeter fell asleep on her bundled cloak within the cave.

Yet I could not. No matter how hard I tried, I could not relax. I hated the low ceiling and the hard floor under me. It made me think about the last time I was in a cave, and after remembering that memory of Zeus and me, I could not rest.

So I crept outside and settled on the forest floor beneath a tree, watching Demeter as she slept within. Yet, despite the night's wind and rain, exhaustion overcame me. I dropped into a sleep in which I dreamed that Zeus was above me again, telling me it would be all right, that I needed to trust him, that I would enjoy it if I just let it happen, and how I was too weak and stupid, too taken by surprise, and too naïve, to stop him.

I woke in a cold sweat, gasping awake, lifting my head off its resting place upon the tree trunk. Then, when I peered into the cave, I saw I was alone — Demeter was gone.

Scrambling to my feet, suddenly awake, I searched the surrounding area for her, calling her name. Panicking, trekking over fallen logs and pushing through bushes, my calls were turning into screams.

"Hera, what are you doing?" Demeter's voice sounded behind me.

I turned around to see her looking at me.

"You ran off," I accused, rushing towards her.

"I woke early. I just went to scout the area." Her voice was quiet.

"Leaving me alone? Something could have attacked me as I slept!"

She did not seem to react to that, for her demeanour was as spiritless as ever. Yet, there was something new, an expression in her eyes, some kind of alarm, almost a warning.

I examined her: her dress was torn; she had lost her cloak; her hair was a tousled mess. "What happened to you?"

"I got caught in some brambles. I had to abandon my cloak. Do you have a spare one?"

I frowned, sensing that she was not being entirely honest. But I did not wish to press her for this was already a trying time. "No. We shall have to stop at a village and find a new one."

She nodded, eyes falling to the ground. "Very well. So be it."

Then, before I asked any more questions, she returned to our little campsite and seemed to avoid all conversation for the rest of the morning.

I observed her over the following hours. Her silent behaviour, guarded yet fragile, was familiar. I had seen it repeatedly but could not quite put my finger on it. I wondered if I had done something to upset her.

Later that day, we came to the town of Eleusis and were welcomed into the palace of the king, Keleus. Dressed as old women, we were referred to the old nurse, Demophon, who crouched as she moved and spoke with a rasp in her voice, yet with wise counsel, too, like most her age. Her role was to aid the queen when caring for the king's infant son, Triptolemos, who was a happy child. Demophon provided everything we needed and spoke much with us about the wild ways of the outdoors and how it was growing more unsafe by the day for ladies of all ages. However, when Demeter saw the infant being neglected, she let him suckle at her own breast, no doubt pining for the loss of her daughter. This caused him to immediately grow into an adult man. Afterwards, she attempted to turn him into a god by anointing him with ambrosia to deify his soul, and to burn away his body on a fire. However, she was stopped by the queen, Mentira, who begged her to let her son live a full life. Demeter did as the mother wished, and offered instead to teach him the art of agriculture, the secrets of a good harvest, so that when he would become king he would know how to feed his people every year.

Leaving Eleusis, wandering through the woodlands, we came across Hekate's tall, lean figure, standing in a clearing with her staff of gems and her wild, divine aura and fire-red untamed hair. She reminded me a little of Athena, wearing an armoured breastplate under her cloak, dressed in a man's tunic and boots.

I recognised her from when we had first arrived in Olympos. Rarely was she ever spotted, yet now, she appeared to us. Much older than even the Titans, she was the first deity outside the Kronides to join our ranks. When Zeus decided her presence threatened his power, she departed Olympos to live a nomadic life of mystery and magic.

"You two cover more ground than me," Hekate remarked, smiling amiably.

"We are in a hurry," I said, trying for a smile in return.

"So I heard," she said, growing serious. "I was sorry to hear of the loss of your daughter, Demeter. I heard she was a beauty."

"She is not dead," my sister corrected her. "Just lost."

"Perhaps she is both," Hekate countered, raising an eyebrow. "Dead. Lost. Same thing."

Demeter huffed. "Is it your intention to waste my time, or do you have some purpose?"

"Indeed. Some information which might help."

"You have waited this long to tell me?"

"I have been trying to find you."

"What news is it?" Demeter snapped impatiently.

The goddess of crossroads recalled: "On that dreadful evening that your dear daughter disappeared, I was traversing the lands outside Olympos when I heard screams coming from the woods like a tortured animal. I did not see who it was, but it sounded like the cries of a maiden. I am afraid I know nothing more."

I glanced at my sister. Her eyes were wide in despair.

"There is someone who might know more," Hekate continued, gesturing to the sky.

We raised our heads, squinting at the sun's midday rays.

"The sun?" I asked aloud.

"Indeed, my lady. Helios is an eternal watcher. He sits higher than any wind, rain, clouds, or Heaven. He sees all that happens below him."

"Can we meet him?"

Hekate frowned. "Not you. Just Demeter. I am afraid he is not fond of Zeus, of being controlled by his descendant, and this disdain extends to his wife."

I pursed my lips, aware of the tension between Zeus and Helios. My husband kept him on a tight leash and never held back from discipline or threats whenever he stepped out of line.

"If Hera does not come with me, I shall not go," Demeter suddenly said.

I turned to her, surprised. "What are you talking about? Helios may have the answer to your daughter's fate."

"Maybe, but he has only chosen to offer his help now, whereas you have been with me all along. This could be a lie, and I shall need another mind to think clearly for me."

She turned to Hekate. "Tell Helios that both Demeter and Hera shall see him."

The goddess of magic huffed. "Tell him yourself."

I frowned. "You are not going to take us to him?"

Hekate raised a red eyebrow. "Do I look like his servant?"

Then she turned to the trees, calling over her shoulder as she disappeared: "Good luck!"

Demeter sighed. "Well, what are we to do now?"

I lifted my nose into the air and felt the warm welcome of the wind. "Hold my hand."

She hesitated, anxiety filling her eyes. "Hera, you know I have vertigo. I hate to be so far from the ground."

I smiled gently. "Then hold on tight unless you have another plan."

Swallowing hard, she let me take the lead for once.

Stepping into the air, I let the wind currents take us past the trees and mountaintops, up to the white and grey clouds, and towards the top of the sky. My heart soared at the same time. We saw Olympos on the way, the grey mountain against the blue sky. We soared as high as we could, the wind blasting our hair and disguises, shaking all weariness from our minds. Demeter cried out often when she glanced down and saw how high up we were. Above the rushing sound of the wind, I roared at her to only look up, for there, just above our heads, was the great golden sun.

The air around us grew hot from the flames. It was as if Helios had reached out across the great emptiness, leading us in. I grew hot and thought I might faint. I briefly thought back to Hephaistos's state after his fall. He was disfigured after his drop from a mountain. So what would happen to us if we fell from the sun's height? I did not have to wonder for long, for a saffron figure came from the massive ball of fire.

Helios emerged from the celestial flames and stared at us, emitting rays of burnt, red fire from his skin. His entire being was as the fire of the sun, which omitted light from every angle and was untouched by shadows. Had we been mortals, we would have burst into flames at sight. As deities, we could just about stand the bright light.

"Lord Helios," I greeted, shouting above the wind. "We are here at the behest of Hekate, who informed us that you —"

"I know what happened to your daughter, Demeter." Helios's mouth barely moved, but his voice was loud, carried by the wind. There was no expression on his face of sun-fire.

"Why have you chosen now to speak of it?" Demeter demanded.

"The King of Heaven would whip me if he knew what I was about to say."

"Where is my daughter?" Demeter asked, panic starting to rise in her voice.

Helios seemed to look out over the cosmos, and then his shoulders heaved. "The princess resides in the farthest place from here," came his reply.

"The realm of Haides?" I asked.

Helios neither nodded nor shook his head. He only said: "It is possible."

Demeter's face grew pale. "How did she get there?"

"Maybe she wandered there. She is quite a curious girl," I suggested.

"One does not simply wander into the Land of the Dead, Queen Hera," Helios snapped at me, spitting out my title.

I blinked, offended. Then I realised the extent of his bitterness towards me, as the wife of the one who was his prison guard, who regulated his every action and beat him if he did as he pleased, who kept him all alone in a fortress of flames. I did not envy him.

"She was taken," he finished, turning to my sister.

Her gaze turned steely. "By whom?"

"I think you know."

"I certainly have a good idea," she hissed. "Kore could not have gone into the Underworld, a goddess, without Haides knowing about it."

A shudder ran up my spine. "I doubt she would have left Heaven without Zeus knowing about it either."

Her grey eyes widened at me, colder than ever before, as she realised what I meant.

"Then my part in this is complete," Helios said. "Leave now. The sky is no place for the goddess of the land." It was an order, but he did not wait to see us depart. Instead, he returned to his home of fire.

Demeter looked at me. "Take me home, Hera. Now."

I nodded. "Of course, but what will we do about this?"

"You do what you wish, but, Chaos help me, I will kill them all."

For her wrath, Demeter was called Erinys, the Avenger.

9: MELAINA

Everyone in the heavenly court of Olympos was astounded when Demeter burst through the council chamber doors, charged straight up to Zeus sitting in his chair at the end of the table, and struck him across the face in front of his entire ministry, and none more so than the king himself. My heart plummeted when I saw it, having rushed in behind her. Yet I think everyone was far more alarmed when she screamed at him, hitting his arms and shoulders in frustration.

"You gave her to Haides without telling me? You jailbird! How dare you! How could you do that to your own daughter!" she exclaimed as she beat him.

Rising from his seat, a scowling Zeus grabbed his sister's flying fists. "Demeter, it was not your decision to make!" His voice boomed out above hers.

He pushed her away from him and brushed down his tunic. "I had no intention of her being stolen away like that. Rest assured Kore will be returned, and the couple will be wed properly. There will be a wedding which the world will witness, a wedding here on Olympos."

Demeter's entire body trembled. "You monster!" she spat, hissing at him.

Zeus bared his teeth and growled: "Don't forget yourself. I am your king."

"And I am a goddess of the earth!" she exploded, saliva flying and her face turning red, veins appearing on her neck. "Mark my words, Zeus. Bring my daughter back to me, or I shall bring drought, and famine to your whole world of precious mortals, and none will pray to you or give you sacrifice. Then I shall bring it here to Mount Olympos and gladly watch as you starve on your throne. Not even sitting in the heights of Heaven could save you from that fate."

Zeus went still, his eyes widening at her.

"Believe me, little brother, there is nothing in the depths of Tartaros or Nyx's constellations above which could make me change my mind to spare what you have spent your life building, not after you have taken my daughter away from me."

Zeus faced her properly. "Demeter, after I sent Haides into slavery, he was outraged. He threatened death on all who lived, even gods. So, I promised him a wife to keep the peace. All he wanted was a bride. I saw no reason to deny him one, and when Kore was born, he wanted her. So, I gave her to him, as is my right."

Demeter grew still.

I understood exactly how she felt. This was the real Zeus: the Zeus who believed that mothers were not parents; the Zeus who only cared about finding Kore because she had been taken in a most unorthodox fashion; the Zeus who only saw the benefit in daughters when they were marriageable.

Her voice was fragile. "Not once in all the years she was under my care did you mention this agreement you had with him, this secret scheme you had to sell my daughter to that toad down in the darkness, where I will never see her again? She was the one good thing I had!"

"She is my daughter too, Demeter, free to be wed as I wish, to whomsoever I wish. Besides, I thought you would be pleased. Haides is the eldest Olympian, the most suitable match for any maiden. She will be the Queen of the Underworld. Do you not want that for her?"

Demeter shook her head, lip wobbling. "I wanted to be involved in the matter and for Kore to have some say in it too."

Zeus scoffed. "You speak as if I did not have her best interest at heart."

The King of Olympos sat back down. "At any rate, Haides had no place to suddenly appear and whisk her away in his chariot like a thief. Hermes is negotiating with our brother as we speak."

He gestured to the ministers around him. "Now, unless there is anything further, we have a lot of work to do."

It took Demeter a moment to give up, but she did, knowing she could not win against the King of Heaven. None of us could.

Demeter sat in silence in her bedchamber. Her eyes were red with tears. She looked defeated, weighed down with grief. When she looked at me, I saw only hopeless despair on her face.

I sat with her, waiting for her to say something.

Then, after a prolonged silence: "How do you do it?" Her voice was quiet and hoarse.

"Do what?"

"Live with him?"

I was slightly taken aback by the question. "I just do, I suppose. I did try to leave, but that also failed." There was more I could have said, but what was the point?

"I never would have lain with him if I thought this would happen," she whispered. "I just wanted another child, to be a mother again. As foolish as it sounds, I never thought Kore would leave me."

"Most mothers can think like this, but fathers often have other plans," I said softly.

She only nodded.

Several days later, Hermes delivered a message to the court from Haides, a declaration that nothing would make the god of the Underworld let Kore leave his realm now that he had her in his keeping. Worse, Haides claimed that the marriage had already been consummated and could not be reversed, making it eternally binding.

Zeus was purple with rage, jumping up from his throne. "That rotten villain! How dare he! The insolence! I will not have it."

He pointed to Hermes. "Return to the Underworld. Tell Haides I shall have my daughter back with no mark on her, or he will have a war on his hands!"

At this point, a madness to speak came over me, in realising Zeus could make a grave mistake and plunge the world into turmoil. So, I said: "My lord."

"What?" he raged, whirling around to face me.

My heart beat fast, but I tried not to tremble under his glare. "Is that sensible?"

He looked as if he would explode.

Quickly, I continued: "Do you think it is possible to win a war against the dead? If Haides has already consummated his marriage with Kore, she is now his wife. She could be pregnant. Taking her from him would only antagonise him further. So, I have an alternative suggestion."

Zeus stared at me momentarily and then sat down with a huff on his throne. "Political counsel from my wife. Go on. No one else seems to have a solution."

I spoke as calmly as I could. "Haides will not come here. He refuses to release Kore. He refuses a wedding on Olympos. So why not bring the wedding to him?"

He frowned. "What do you mean?"

"Haides's isolation in the Underworld has caused him to forget much. He must feel very safe down there, believing himself untouchable, but this is untrue. The way is not barred for gods — Hermes proves that every day. We are simply not welcome. Let this be no barrier to us now. Meet with Haides yourself. Bring the Kronides together. Talk some sense into him. Punish him if necessary. Moreover, if we can convince him to show us Kore, I can check if he has had a full union with her and if she is bearing his child. If not, we may still bring her home. If he has, we can convince Haides to say his vows in front of his family so we can recognise her as his wife."

Zeus looked away, seeming displeased.

"It may not be the ideal situation, but diplomacy is required now to salvage Kore's virtue and to teach Haides that he cannot steal souls whenever he wishes. If we do not act, he will only grow more rebellious."

A silence descended on the court as we all awaited the king's response.

He took a moment, and then he nodded. "Very well. Let us organise an embassy to go to Haides and take back Persephone."

There was no applause at his words, no cheering, no hope. This was a quest to the Land of the Dead, where not even gods had much sway.

Poseidon soon arrived on Olympos, having been summoned to participate in our plan, dressed in a cloak of dark seaweed adorned with shells, with a high crown of shells and gems, and clams at the base.

I embraced him eagerly, pleased to see my brother again. He returned the affection.

We all sat down and devised what to say and how to handle the meeting with Haides. It was going to be a surprise visit, we decided. If Haides knew we were coming, he might put up physical barriers around the Underworld, making our mission impossible. We agreed that Demeter and I would determine the state of Kore's maidenhood. At the same time, Zeus and Poseidon would admonish their elder brother. Then depending on whether or not they had consummated the marriage, there would be a wedding, and Zeus would hold Haides in place until he said his marriage vows, no matter how long it took. If they had not, we would simply smuggle Kore out the way we came.

That night, I decided to check on Demeter as she had remained silent throughout all the discussions. I knew that she wanted her daughter to be back home on Olympos, but there would be a union unless Kore was somehow set free by Haides. Demeter would have to accept that. But I also knew she resented Zeus, possibly even more so than Haides. She often locked herself away, too angry to be around people. I knocked on her door.

She opened it. Her hair was a long, scraggly mess, her eyes red and puffy from crying. She was in her nightdress, with a shawl wrapped around her, wearing none of the fineries that Zeus had gifted her. No doubt, after all she had been through, she found his gifts repugnant.

"Oh, dear sister," I sighed. "How dreadful you look."

I closed the door behind us, following her into her bedchamber. "Why not go for a walk? You might feel better after."

"I am not leaving this room, not with him out there."

"Zeus is in the throne room, nowhere near your quarters," I reassured her.

She closed her eyes and shook her head. "No, not him. Poseidon."

I was confused. "What do you mean?"

She hesitated and then looked at me. "I am pregnant, Hera, with Poseidon's child." Her voice was shaking.

It was the last thing I expected her to say. "What?" I laughed, assuming it was a jest.

"I am pregnant. The child is Poseidon's," she repeated, her cheeks wet. "I do not know what to do."

I sat down on the bed; my legs were weak, and I felt winded. "I do not understand."

She sniffled as she wiped her cheeks. "On our travels, there was a night when I awoke while you were sleeping. I needed to relieve myself. As I was walking, I was attacked by someone. I recognised Poseidon's voice although it was too dark to see him. I managed to get away. I ran to a farm nearby and transformed into a horse to blend in with the other animals, but that did not trick him for he created the creature. He just turned into a stallion, did what he wanted, and left. I found a spring nearby. I tried to wash him off me, the little good it did."

I surged to my feet. I recalled the moment well. I had known something was amiss, but I had not been able to put my finger on it. The fact that she had cleaned herself afterwards would have made it difficult to figure out. "Why did you not tell me?"

"I was ashamed. I felt so dirty."

"Demeter, I would have done anything. I am your sister."

We stood in silence for a few moments.

I reached out to hold her hands. "I just wish there was something I could do."

"Help me deliver the baby and then give it to Poseidon," she replied, a stern determination coming over her face.

"You shall not keep it yourself?"

"Do you think Zeus would let it live here on Olympos? Would he do that if you had someone else's child? Even if he did, he would force you to raise it, not me!"

I knew she was right, so I asked no more questions.

On my way back to my chambers, Poseidon was in the hallway. I heard his laughter before his footsteps or saw his smirking face, so self-assured as he spoke to a courtier. An impulse overtook my senses. Approaching, I grabbed his wrist, yanking him away from his conversation, and pulled him down a side passage of the palace.

"Hera, what are you doing?" he asked, baffled.

I turned to him, ichor boiling. "I know what you did."

"Know what?"

"About Demeter," I hissed.

He rolled his eyes. "Always so dramatic with you, Hera. We just had sex."

"Demeter claims not to have consented to any such thing."

He frowned and shrugged. "Does she have to? Sometimes these things happen naturally."

At that, my palm flew across his face before I could stop myself.

Shocked, he stumbled back, holding a hand to his cheek.

"First Zeus. Then Haides. Now you," I spat. "Will it ever end?"

He glowered. "Stop it!"

"I expect that's what she thought. You attacked her," I spat at him. "She fled, but still you pursued, trapped, and used her. Deny it all you want, but I know what a disgusting little —"

Suddenly his hand was on my throat, pushing me up against the wall. "Shut up," he said. "I do not have to take this slander from you."

"What are you going to do? Take me as well?"

He chuckled at the challenge. "If I did?"

"Zeus would rip you apart," I hissed quietly. "You would be little more than dead." Whatever Zeus's abuses towards me, I knew he would defend my honour with all he had.

Poseidon's jaw hardened, the light dying from his eyes.

"Get away from me," I snapped.

He let go, glaring down at me.

"Tread carefully, little sister," he warned. "Recall that I am the only one of the Olympians who knows the true extent of your escapades. How would Zeus react if he knew you had spent weeks in the court of Okeanos?"

How he had come to find that out, I knew not. Maybe Okeanos had told him, or some spy in the underwater court. It didn't matter now. I shrugged, knowing Zeus better than him. "Remove your threats, Poseidon. As far as I see it, Zeus would only bring his wrath upon you for not telling him sooner and bringing me home. Indeed, he might also wonder why Okeanos was the one to save me, and you were not! So, go ahead. Tell Zeus everything you wish, but I fear it would not have the effect you want." I turned away from him, feeling strength flow through me.

Not long after that, Demeter went into labour and delivered two children: Despoina, the goddess of nature, a beautiful baby girl, and Arion, a black horse who would be the fastest steed in the known world. One can imagine our expressions when I pulled the horse out of my sister's womb. I brought the children to Poseidon's chambers and gave them to a somewhat baffled nymph. I know not where the children went from there but Despoina grew to be a beautiful maiden and, in time, Arion proved himself to be so swift he was assigned to Herakles before he was made a god.

In time, the story of Demeter's suffering at Poseidon's hands, for which she would be called Demeter Melaina, or Demeter the Black, would be broadcast far and wide. It reached the ears of a mortal named Hierax, who abandoned the worship of Poseidon in favour of Demeter, building sanctuaries for her. In return, she sent him bountiful harvests. Poseidon, in his jealousy, flooded the crops, but it never stopped Demeter from making them grow. She never let Poseidon have his way with her again.

10: PERSEPHONE

It was not just a rescue mission to bring Kore home. Our whole world was on the cusp of war and annihilation should the dead meet the living on the battlefield and the divine get caught in the middle. Whatever the Moirai had in mind, the rapture of Persephone could become a combat of a magnitude even beyond that of the Titanomachy.

Leaving Olympos and descending to the Earth's surface, the Kronides went to Delphi, the centre of Hellas. Demeter commanded rocks in the ground to split open. The Kronides went through, led by Hermes, familiar with the steep road into the dark depths. Zeus was next. Demeter followed him, with Hestia and me behind her. There had been some debate about whether Hestia should leave Olympos, a matter I decided to stay out of – having Hestia anywhere near me was still cause for contention. Still, it was eventually agreed that all the Kronides had to go if our presence was to have the most potent effect on Haides. Finally, Poseidon brought up the rear.

We had wondered whether or not to bring the rest of the Olympian family, but it was deemed too unsafe. Precautions had been taken. In Zeus's absence, Ares would govern Olympos, if only to declare war on Haides if something happened to us: Olympos would have the best chance of winning with him at the helm, with Hephaistos equipping our troops and with Athena training them in the art of war and battle strategy. Aphrodite would lead any peace process required, as she possessed the best chance of bringing Haides to surrender or to agree to a treaty.

The Underworld is a foul place. I smelled the despair of the dead wafting through the rocks before I even stepped through them. Then I heard the agonised screams of those in the Fields of Punishment rising up to the Earth's surface and the lost wails of those in the Fields of Asphodel, bemoaning their sorry state. Behind the rocks, a red glow filled the darkness within, coming from below, and Zeus put his lightning bolt away. Peering over the ledge on which we were carefully walking, I saw the Kingdom of Haides.

The river Styx, the largest river I had ever seen, cut straight through the black landmass, along which a single warship ran its course: the ferry of Charon, which delivered dead souls to the gateway of the kingdom at the mouth of the river, and where the gargantuan three-headed hound, Kerberos, guarded the kingdom against unwelcome visitors and hunted down any wretched souls trying to escape. Behind the gate stood Haides's palace, an enormous, intimidating fortress much more significant than our palace of Olympos — made entirely from onyx obsidian, with numerous lofty towers and high roofs. Torchlight lit it up from the inside, looking like it was on fire from within. It was a desolate place, ghostly and gloomy, a shadowy world of waste and collapse, a place of hopelessness. The air was laced with grief and anger. The ground was dust, falling apart beneath our feet.

Beyond the palace walls on either side lay the Fields of Asphodel, a vast desolate land of undulating hills and scattered houses, with nothing growing save for small dark bitter flowers, the food of the dead. It is here ordinary folk go when they die. Towards the mountains behind the palace, we saw the Fields of Punishment, separated from the rest of the kingdom by a large metal gate. This is where souls receive retribution for their crimes from the Erinyes, nymphs of vengeance, children of darkness and night. Then we heard the most tortured noises possible. They seemed so near it was terrifying. I knew these were emanating from the yawning, gaping hole of Tartaros where all the worst sorts of monsters dwell, the evilest and most vengeful of all being the Titans, just waiting for the day of reckoning when they will have their revenge on the Olympians and all the poor souls who supported them.

I turned and, out to sea, beyond the river mouth, saw the Elysian Fields, with torches lighting it up in the darkness as it glowed in its white marble walls. I caught the faint sound of music — drums, flutes, and lyres. I had even heard that sometimes the sun shines there. Those whose lives are extraordinary or exceptionally pious revel across that land. Finally, in the distance, to the far west, out where the onyx sea becomes a sapphire ocean, are the Isles of the Blessed lying in perpetual sunshine. I could not see them but knew they were there, only ever seen by those distinguished enough to have been reborn three times in their lives each time they entered the Elysian Fields. It is said they are beautiful with exotic woodlands of radiant colours that exist in no other place, even more beautiful than Olympos, which is hard to believe. Those who make it this far go to paradise, to a blessed life of eternal happiness. However, the rest was darkness and despair and death.

I froze, suddenly overcome with terror. It was as if all the sorrow and fury of every soul in the Underworld had risen within me. The idea of being in such a place as this made me petrified. I knew I should not be here. I knew it was not right. Every part of me told me to flee. Being in Okeanos' world had been uncomfortable enough, but this was much stronger.

"What are you doing, Hera?" Poseidon demanded in my ear.

The others ahead halted and looked back to see what was going on.

Zeus scowled. "Come, Hera. There is no time to delay."

I swallowed hard, knowing I should obey, but I could not. I could not take another step of my own free will. My heart began to race inside my breast. Glancing past Poseidon's glowering face, I saw the closed rocks behind us from where we had entered. I could not see the sun anymore.

"Can you not see she is afraid?" Hestia snapped at them. "Let her return if she wishes."

I knew I looked weak, but I did not care. I was cold and trembling. I thought I would lose control, faint, or have some kind of heart attack.

Then Poseidon huffed and gave me a shove. "Come on."

I stumbled forwards.

Zeus reached back and grabbed my wrist, hauling me to his side. He growled in my ear: "My queen cannot be the only deity to fear death."

After that, I had no choice but to swallow my fear and continue further into the Land of the Dead. I did my best to ignore my anxiety, but with every step, it worsened. Then I silently scolded myself: What did I have to fear from this place? Why did I fear this place?

Our pathway came to form part of the mountain landscape, and we descended into the Fields of Asphodel. The dead souls we passed parted for us, seeming surprised to see us. Unlike mortals, they did not bow or appear in awe. They just stared. They had nothing to fear, not even us. It was unnerving, and I was not the only one who did not like it. In a way, the dead were like us now — they were eternal but eternally powerless. I could see that Zeus was apprehensive. I wondered if he regretted that he made Prometheus create all those centuries ago. Was all the worship from humans worth it when one was just creating enemies in the afterlife, bitter at the gods for not answering their prayers? If Haides ever raised his soul to the Earth's surface, humans would not stand a chance and would join his ranks. If war was to break out, it would never end.

After a winding and anxious journey, we reached the back gate into Haides's palace. Zeus knocked on the gates, which were opened by a nymph, the likes of which I had never seen before, a grey creature, shrivelled and shrunken, no higher than my hip, bald with beady eyes, sharp teeth, and tunic in tatters. It just looked at us and then turned away, leaving the gate open, giving us little choice but to follow.

Passing through Haides's palace was just as strange. It was beautiful in its own way. Down we went through black labyrinthine corridors, twisting and turning, disorientating. They were lined with torches while gems and precious stones were embedded in the rock.

We did not pass anyone else along the way — so different from the bustling court at Olympos — walking in constant fear at what might be lying in wait around the next corner. Still, it was just more of what went before. I could not shake the feeling that I was being watched or that we were simply seeing what Haides wanted us to see. We did not know what to expect in this land — there were no rules here other than the fate of one's soul, the decision of its eternal resting place left to Haides and his council of judges. There was nothing familiar here.

At last, we came to two large stone doors. The nymph pushed them open and led us to what we soon realised was the throne room. It was black, just like the rest of the palace, but with large columns stretching up to a ceiling clouded in shadow. Gemstones and precious metals had been melted down, twisted into various designs, and placed along the walls, interspersed with torches of light and souls, all staring at us. I recognised among their faces famous rulers who had died. I realised that this was Haides's court: a gathering of those who would have been the wealthiest and most influential minds on Earth when they were alive, those too good to send to the Fields of Asphodel but not heroic enough to be sent to the Elysian Fields. Some faces even made me blush, including Princess Semele's gaze, peering out from behind other heads. Beside her stood Queen Europa of Krete, who had parted me from my daughter, Angelia. I ignored them.

A purple carpet lined an aisle towards a small staircase, at the top of which was Haides's throne, which seemed to be built into the stone itself, in hues so dull and dreary that it seemed like an ominous presage of the eternity to come for most souls. Then my eyes landed upon my eldest brother.

Haides sat on his throne, dressed unsurprisingly in black and with an obsidian crown. It shimmered in the torchlight like a lake in the moonlight. He had grown into his position. He had fully embraced his power here. It was impressive. As disgusted with him as I was for what he had done to Kore, I realised oddly that I was proud of what he had built here. One could not help but be both impressed and intimidated.

He raised his arms in welcome. "Greetings, brothers and sisters. Welcome to my home. Come forward. Let me see you all."

And so, we obliged the King of the Underworld. I noticed a flush on Zeus's face. He did not like being beckoned, like a dog to its master.

Haides lowered his hands, and his smile faded. "I must say this is quite a surprise. What brings you all here today? I received no warning that we were to have a family reunion."

"You stole my daughter," Demeter hissed through bared teeth. Her fists were clenched by her sides, her knuckles so white it was as if she was ready to lunge forward and strangle him.

Haides sighed. "Straight to business, I see."

He stood up and began to descend the steps, his descent echoing around the obsidian hall. "My dear sister, I never meant to cause any harm or distress, certainly not to Kore, my wife. Zeus, our baby brother, gave me permission to take her as my wife. In fact, since he knew you would disagree, Zeus even suggested that I take her in the way I did."

My heart sank. I stared at Zeus, who had turned his gaze to the ground in embarrassment. I was horrified that he had not only allowed Haides to capture Kore and take her from her family but had encouraged it. Worse still, he had shamelessly lied about it. Perhaps that part was not so shocking.

Demeter grew still and closed her eyes. When she opened them, her glare was far more piercing than before.

"So, I took her. Once Kore understood why, she was happy to oblige without a fuss."

"Liar!" Demeter snapped. "Hekate heard her screams. Helios saw how she tried to run away and how you snatched her, kicking and flailing, onto your chariot."

"It was incredibly alarming," Zeus agreed, raising an eyebrow at Haides. "Why the need for dramatics, brother? You would have had her eventually. You just needed to be patient."

"I have been patient for a long time, little brother," Haides snarled. "You promised me a wife. You swore on the Styx. You cannot deny me her now."

"We do not come to take her away from you if you have already made her your wife. We merely require a ceremony to see you both together. Demeter wishes to see her daughter. She never even got the chance to say goodbye."

Haides looked at each of us in turn. "Is that all?"

We all nodded. It was part of the plan.

"I would be happy to preside," I added. "Why not make this a joyous occasion, dear brother? We wish you all the best in your marriage. We just ask you to treat Kore as any bride. Let her father give her away. Let her mother prepare a bridal chamber. Where is the harm in that?"

He pursed his lips and looked carefully at Demeter. "This is truly what you want?"

It must have taken much strength for her to nod and agree, but she did.

"May we see her?" I asked. "May we prepare her for the ceremony?"

He smiled. "Of course. Let me reassure you that any notion you might have of whisking her away while my brothers distract me will be in vain."

There was silence among the group.

I coughed slightly, trying to laugh. "We are not here to trick you, Haides."

He chuckled too. "Good, because even if you got her as far as the rocks whence you came, you would still fail in your attempt."

Demeter could not help herself. "Why?"

He blinked innocently at her. "Kore has been here for ten days now. As a living creature, she has to eat. She has become particularly fond of the pomegranates grown in my gardens. She has been eating them gladly. You all know Chaos's cosmic law."

Victory seeped into his gaze. He could not keep the triumphant grin off his face.

Dread came over me.

Zeus muttered a curse under his breath. Poseidon shook his head, disgusted with the actions of his eldest brother. Hestia sucked in an anxious breath. As for Demeter, she continued to stare at Haides, expressionless.

We all knew the law: living mortal bodies who stayed in the Underworld long enough to have to eat from it could never leave, having committed themselves to it. They were as good as dead themselves.

Haides smirked. "Have I said something?"

Demeter stood rigidly still, fuming. "I do not care about the bloody cosmic law. She is my daughter. I will have her back, or you will have hell on your hands."

"Is that truly your threat?" Haides snorted. "I deal with hell every day. It is my job."

She laughed. "On the contrary, it is your job to keep a grip on the realm you have. It is your job to organise and house millions of dead and depressed souls, to keep them as happy as possible. That number will only grow, and perhaps the kingdom could expand to accommodate it. Still, I do not think it could handle tripling its population in a matter of days, could it? You certainly could not. The Earth can only hold so many humans at once. I imagine the realm of the dead is much the same."

Haides's face darkened. "What are you saying?"

It was now Demeter's turn to smirk, but it quickly turned ugly. "Give me back my daughter, pregnant or not, or watch this cosmos combust. The land will wither and die. Calamity will ensue. In a matter of weeks, there shall not be a world left for the living and no one to worship the divine, including you. As for this place, it will be overrun. Tartaros will burst open from the flood. Is your power really that strong to keep so many in check?"

"Demeter," Hestia said slowly. "You would bring an apocalypse."

Our sister nodded with her chin high. "It has already started. Famine has begun to spread throughout Hellas. It will not be long until your halls are flooded. This world shall not last a month."

The Kronides brothers stared at her, floored by her words.

Haides nodded. "Well spoken, sister," he acknowledged. But there was a steeliness in his eyes. "If it is chaos you want, it is chaos you shall get."

He turned around and began to walk back up to his throne. He drew a colossal iron key from underneath his cloak. He inserted it into a central hole above it. He opened a secret door in the obsidian wall, dragging it open with dust and a screeching sound flying into the air. A new cold blasted through into the throne room, a wind from a place that did not know the sun's heat.

Stepping forward, I peered into the darkness of the river Styx. I had expected to see the Fields of Asphodel, but this was a view to the other side of the river, away from Haides's settlement, onto a land of vast darkness. I could make out the chasm in the rock, the void stretching down even further to the Earth's core, full of the sound of persecution and misery. The realisation came over me, and I moved away quickly from the window. I could feel the resentment, the gazes staring back at me from the schism of Tartaros. What lay in the rock was ready to leap out and eat everything in its path. I knew that Kronos was down there with his Titans. The primordial gods only knew what other foul creatures lurked in the great chasm, waiting to climb out.

Haides looked down upon Demeter. "Remove your threats, or I will release the Titans and let them devour your precious Earth in minutes."

"Do that, and I shall stop everything down here from growing: every plant, tree, root, and pulse. Your dead souls might survive. However, I doubt you will, and it will certainly destroy Persephone. You can watch her starve while you waste away, and you will forever regret bringing you both to the same fate," Demeter replied. She did not scream, rage, or cry. She was earnest, determined, and unmoving. "I would rather see her destroyed than never see her again. You would only have her body for company when she lies a lifeless corpse. I would let the soil take her under this place, far away from you. I shall turn her into nothing just as quickly as I brought her to life."

Haides's face went slack. "You would not dare."

"Stop, both of you!" Zeus bellowed.

"This is madness," Hestia muttered, her eyes brimming with tears.

I stepped forward to Haides, hoping to appeal to him. I took his hand in mine, desperately hoping my words would have some effect. I wanted to resolve this issue and leave this forsaken place. I stared pityingly into his dark eyes. "Haides, listen to me. Do not pretend you did not know what scandal would happen when you took Kore away. You have been locked down here for centuries. The first chance of the light again, you took. You did not want to wait for a wedding day. You had run out of patience. You live every day in a place where no one understands you. Of course, you want a wife and should have one with everyone's blessing. You must be allowed to have a companion who will love you and care for you and give you a family. I am delighted you saw the benefit of a wife. Yet you should not have done it like this. All it has achieved is turmoil and strife in your family, those who love you."

He scoffed. "Spare me the sentiment."

I drew back slightly, offended. "You think we do not care for you? I do. I also think that Kore could love you too, but you must treat her well. Taking her away from her mother, like a bandit, terrifying her and forcibly keeping her here was never going to achieve that."

I gestured back to Demeter. "All our sister wants is to see that her daughter is well."

He glanced warily at her. "No, she wishes to end this marriage in its entirety."

I turned to her. "If you were to be able to visit Persephone whenever you wanted, to see her, spend time with her, and stay with her, would you seriously object to her match with Haides if you could see him treating Kore well? Would it truly be so bad to share her? She was going to be married one day."

Demeter shuffled on her feet. "I suppose not," she muttered.

I turned back to Haides. "Give Demeter the same access that Hermes has to this place."

"I cannot have gods coming and going whenever they please," he said stubbornly.

I tried not to let my frustration show. "Do you honestly believe Kore will be happy being kept away from her family forever? No wife or even mistress would stand for that."

Haides was silent for a while, looking at me. Then something in his expression changed. His eyes softened, and he sighed, looking down in shame. "Kore is not my wife nor my mistress. I wanted her to be willing. I want her to be happy. When I saw her, I was enchanted. I had a moment of madness. I could not help myself. I am sorry," he whispered.

I imagined it was not easy for him to be so open with those he had not been near for a long time. He seemed truthful.

"So, what do you suggest?" Demeter cut in, her tone hard.

He looked at her. "I would allow her to visit you on Earth for a certain time every year."

"Nine months?" Demeter asked.

He frowned. "I was thinking of two."

"Seven."

"Four."

"Six," I suggested. "Half and half."

Haides looked displeased. "It is a long time away from her husband."

"I would hardly advocate infidelity, brother," Demeter snapped.

"Why do we not ask Kore? Does she not deserve to have some say?" I asked.

My brothers looked at me blankly.

I huffed, addressing Haides. "Surely, if you want her to be happy, she must be content with the terms of your marriage. After scaring the girl, you owe her that."

He hesitated and then nodded. Then he took us to Kore.

The princess seemed in good health, if not a bit plumper than when I had last seen her. Looking around her bedchamber, it was evident she had everything she needed. Dressed in a delicate linen gown with a silk grey shawl, wearing fine colourful gems mined in the Underworld, she eagerly embraced her mother with tears of relief and joy. But when she asked if she was being taken home, Haides and I turned away to let Demeter explain the agreement.

Then Haides came before Kore.

"My lady, first let me apologise with my whole heart for how I have treated you. It is my earnest desire to be with you in matrimony, and should you agree I will spend the rest of our eternity together making up for it. I want you to be happy. Queen Hera has suggested you spend half the year with me and half with your mother above. Here you will be free to roam as you wish, save for Tartaros. The gardens are yours and I would ask that you plant in them as much as you can, starting with these."

Holding up in the palm of his hand, he presented Kore with golden apple seeds. I had brought them as a blessing for Kore, seeds from the Tree of Life, growing in the Land of the Dead. I had decided to give them to Haides as a gesture of goodwill.

"A token of my love," he muttered, blushing.

Kore seemed swayed by his words. Perhaps she was naive, but her tendency to see the good in everyone was a trait she would always possess. So she gladly accepted the seeds, the terms of their marriage, and even said that she looked forward to their time together. She then reached up on her tiptoes and planted a light kiss on his cheek.

That evening, the court of the dead came together for the wedding. Haides and Kore said their vows, and festivities ensued. The dancing of the Underworld was not the lively activity we were used to in Olympos. The music was more profound and slower than on Earth. It was more sensual. The dead danced in pairs, pressed close together until they almost kissed. Courtiers danced like they had all the time in the world, which I supposed they did. The bride and groom made their speeches. Kore shed her pet name, reclaiming the true one she had been given at birth: Persephone, Queen of the Underworld.

One guest at the wedding called Minthe, a Naiad of the river Kokytus, made a spectacle of herself by insulting the bride behind her back, saying she was more beautiful than

Persephone, that Haides would tire of her and return to her bed instead. She predicted he would expel his new bride from his palace and leave her to rot in the deadlands outside. Demeter overheard this and confronted her about it. It later transpired that Haides had kept her as a mistress before his betrothal to Persephone. Still, once he secured his engagement, he cast her aside. I admit I was impressed by Haides's ready devotion to his bride. True to her nature, Demeter transformed Minthe into a plant that would forever become known as mint, ready to spread its vicious roots everywhere. When I asked my sister why, she said she had learned something from me: while husbands could be unreliable, there would still be females who would gladly welcome their attention, no matter who it hurt.

I was also reunited briefly with my daughter Angelia at that time. She was full-grown now, a tall, beautiful young goddess with ivy-green eyes and fair hair. She stood out like a spectre in the realm of Haides, always donning white, a sign of her purity from being bathed in the River Acherusia. We embraced tightly, spent many hours talking, and danced until the celebrations ended. It was the only moment in the world of the dead that relieved me from the pains of angst in my chest.

Looking at Persephone and Haides dancing together in a slow-moving rhythm, embraced tightly, gracefully gliding across the floor, I could not help but think that despite a rocky start, it was a happy ending for the couple. In fact, it was the most perfect marriage I could have envisaged. Persephone was, in many ways, free to do what she wanted when in her husband's home and could roam the Earth to see all her other friends and family, while Haides did not take a mistress now that he had a wife. He seemed determined to make his bride happy. I could not help but think it was the marriage that I should have had.

After the wedding, Demeter spread the word about marriage worldwide. It came to pass that Persephone's comings and goings from the Underworld, in line with Demeter's happiness, would cause the seasons to come into being, with the start of spring to the end of the harvest being when they were together. The mortals created the Eleusinian Mysteries, a great festival held twice a year at Eleusis that celebrated the secrets of everlasting life and rebirth, with Persephone's return considered a kind of resurrection. In time, when grown, her half-sister Despoina became Mistress of the Mysteries at the same festival.

It took my sister much time to move past the injury that had been done to her. She punished Ascalaphos, the guardian of Haides's orchard, for not stopping Persephone from eating the pomegranate seeds. She crushed him underneath a rock. When Herakles later came to the Underworld and freed him, she turned Ascalaphos into an owl. She continued to want to be a mother, so she reared the mortal Orthopolis, who would become the twelfth king of the kingdom of Sicyon in Hellas. She also raised Trophonios, a prophetic son of Apollo. Finally, she bore a son called Philomenos, who invented the plough. He was immortalised in the night sky after his death for his ingenious creation. But all of that goodness came from his mother, from Demeter.

11: ZYGIA

With no more distractions, such as my absence from the court and a kidnapped princess, the wedding of Hephaistos and Aphrodite got underway. The entire city was decorated for the event. Parades were held up and down the streets in a spectacular festival. The Muses played throughout the day in the grand dining hall. On the morning of the big day, mortals on Earth made sacrifices and libations in honour of the event, which the engaged couple gladly received.

Since Aphrodite did not know of her true mother, Dione, it was my duty to act as her mother. I was obliged to wake her, dress her, and prepare her bridal chamber.

Unsurprisingly, she was hostile throughout the proceedings. First, she refused to leave her bed even after being brought breakfast. It took my sisters and me to yank her into a seated position. Then she chewed her food slowly, so frustratingly slothfully that we decided to do her makeup and hair while she was in bed. I tried not to let her attitude bother me. Still, I would be lying if I did not say I took some annoyance out on her scalp as I brushed and tugged, reflecting on how she would have an advantageous, prosperous, and faithful union with someone who truly loved her, a blessing few had.

"Ouch," she cried, reaching her hand back to touch her head. "That hurts."

I huffed. "If you like, we can shave it off as the Spartan women do. Would that help?"

At that, she stopped complaining. Then Aphrodite seemed to grow resigned to the reality of her situation. She rose from the bed on my command. She was beautified, with her hair lifted high off her shoulders in braids around her head and rouge making her complexion glow with rosy tones. She did not look at anyone as she was undressed. She let herself be led to a bronze bath, her body doused in water and oils. She did not look anyone in the eyes as she was dressed in her bridal clothes, a white dress bound tightly around her waist with a rope belt and a sunset saffron veil draped over her face, clasped at her collarbone by a golden brooch. We layered her with beaded jewellery and gems wherever possible. Demeter had made a flower crown of pink roses to put on Aphrodite's head. At last, she was ready.

I stood before her.

She stared at the ground, refusing to look at me. Her jaw was clenched, her fury seemingly reserved for me.

I ignored this and carried out the next part of my duties. "Aphrodite, we shall now escort you to the great hall where there shall be a luncheon feast followed by dancing and wedding hymns. Then there shall be a chariot procession where you will travel with Hephaistos to my temple on Olympos. Zeus shall give you to Hephaistos before the altar. There will be a sacrifice, which Zeus will make in honour of your union to Gaia and Ouranos, followed by your vows. Then you shall return to the palace where you shall consummate your marriage. The next morning, gifts shall be given. Do you have any questions?"

She shook her head.

"Then let us depart," I said, nodding to the others.

Aphrodite did not eat at the feast, despite the mountain of food Hephaistos eagerly passed to her, himself dressed in his most delicate cloak and his black hair adorned with a bright green garland, scrubbed clean of all soot from his forges and furnace. She consented to one shaky dance with her limping husband-to-be, but sat down for the rest of the merriment. She refused anything from anyone else and ignored me throughout the afternoon. Hephaistos, in his happiness, seemed content to look at her and let her be.

Then, at the invitation of Zeus, she found the courage to walk toward the chariot, where Hephaistos helped her on board. They rode steadily to the temple, the court of Olympos following behind. Zeus handed her to Hephaistos before the altar. After that, a lamb was sacrificed to Ouranos and Gaia. Then I, Zygia, the goddess of unions, conducted the ceremony. Aphrodite gazed at the ground with tears in her eyes while Hephaistos beamed up at me. After pronouncing them married, I returned to the palace where I took torches in my hands, ready to receive the newly wedded couple. Upon their return, I was obliged to hand her a ripe fruit — I chose an apple as Aphrodite was fond of them — and say, "May you bear my son many children to come."

Still, she did not look at me.

Then the bride and groom were taken separately to their bridal chamber. His closest friends led Hephaistos out, their entourage excitedly shouting and whooping, with my son grinning from ear to ear. Aphrodite was escorted in silence and speed by my sisters and my daughters. They reached the bridal chamber simultaneously from either side of the corridor. Hermes was massaging Hephaistos's shoulders as they approached as if gearing him up to enter a duel.

I opened the door and gestured for them to enter. I saw all the colour drain from Aphrodite's face. For the first time, she looked at me in desperation and terror. My heart sank as I stared back at her, fully understanding what I was forcing her to do. Whatever would happen next, I would be just as much to blame as Hephaistos.

"Ladies first," Hephaistos said, gesturing for her to enter.

Her gaze fell to the floor. She moved silently inside.

Hephaistos's friends clapped him on the back as they left, wishing him luck.

Laughing, my son was about to go inside after his bride when I grabbed his wrist, my heart pounding. He stopped in his tracks and looked at me. "Yes, Mother?"

My mouth was dry. I knew there was very little I could do to stop this. If I prevented Hephaistos from entering, I would break his heart and ruin my relationship with him forever. However, if I let him follow Aphrodite, I would break her heart and destroy my bond with her, if I had not already done that.

"Is everything all right?" he asked. He put a hand on my shoulder as if I might need help.

My eyes stung. "Just be kind to her," I whispered.

He looked surprised. "Of course. Why would I not? I love her."

I nodded. "Yes." I could not bring myself to smile.

"I shall see you in the morning," he said, leaning in and kissing me.

He then turned around and went through the door, closing it after him.

Athena's voice then spoke up: "I thank the Moirai every day that I am not married."

Artemis shivered in agreement.

I stood at the door for a few moments, wondering whether or not to go inside and stop them. I wish I had. But my pride got in the way, and I kept my word to Hephaistos.

12: APHRODITE

The world celebrated their union because the goddess of love was finally married. Many were divided as to whether or not beauty should be paired with ugliness. I hoped Aphrodite would become, at the very least, fond of her husband. I also hoped that Hephaistos would remain too pleased to notice her lack of love for him and, if he ever did, remain patient with her and steadfast in his kindness.

My son entered the marriage infatuated, head over heels in love. He wanted nothing more than to be with her, make her happy, and have her feel the same joy and delight he did when together. It was not to be. The flame of her spirit dwindled. She could often be seen alone or waving her hands exasperatedly in her husband's face. Some woodland nymphs reported seeing her weeping by a brook in the forest. I was unsure when Hephaistos first realised that Aphrodite was not as smitten with him as he was with her. As the solitude and separation dragged on and on, his elation and pleasure at his marriage to this beautiful goddess turned to profound unhappiness, followed by, inevitably, bitter regret.

I felt guilty about it all. I really did. I had never wanted either of them to be unhappy. I often visited Hephaistos at his forge on Mount Olympos, where he retreated most of the time. He had learned not to search for Aphrodite for fear of embarrassing himself in public when confronting her, for she would turn his jealousy back on him. Meanwhile, what he feared most was that Aphrodite had become a traitor to their union. Indeed, rumours flew about the court about her various exploits, that the goddess of love had become an adulteress, an object of lust and rash passion.

Hephaistos's forge lay at the end of the city. On one such visit, I walked through the streets, carrying a basket of fresh fruit — he did not eat well these days. As I strolled along, courtiers and citizens bowed and curtseyed in my direction, halting their steps as they did so. The houses and temples began to slope down the mountainside, beyond the city's boundaries, into the woods' edge. I had to step over fallen branches, and past brambles before I came to trees bowed into a natural arch in front of a large slab of rock in the mountainside, behind which my son's smithy workshop lay, a cave in the mountain itself.

Knocking on the great stone, the magic which coated its existence rolled it to the side, creating a gap for me to enter through. I stepped into the dimness and walked down a dark stone tunnel lit with blazing torches. A wooden door was at the end of this tunnel. Turning the handle, I pushed it open and went inside.

Hephaistos's workshop was, as usual, filled with smoke. One could not help but choke upon entry; the windows did not let in enough fresh air to the thick grey haze within. A layer of grease and ash coated all the surfaces, including the floor. Usually, nymphs would be hard at work at the anvils or the furnaces, doing whatever it was that smithies did — I usually tried not to stay too long to have matters explained to me, or my throat would begin to get raspy, and my eyes would start to water — but this time, the place felt abandoned.

After becoming accustomed to the smell and thickness of the ashy air, I searched for my son among the equipment. I saw him at the back of the workshop, sitting at a desk, fiddling with some golden rope in his hands, weaving it tightly around iron rods. I smiled and approached, putting the basket of fruit down on a nearby table.

"Hello, Mother," he muttered, noting my presence but not looking up from his work.

"Hello, my dear," I replied. "How are you faring? Where are your workers?"

"I sent them home today," he mumbled in reply. "I am working on a personal project."

I nodded, curious. "What is it?"

"A gift for my wife."

I frowned, staring at the rope before him. "Do you think Aphrodite will like it?"

"Well if she doesn't, I will."

I blinked, surprised. However, Hephaistos did not explain further. I looked for things to comment on. I turned my head towards the window and saw what Hephaistos had feared all these years. In the woods beyond were Ares and Aphrodite, sprawled across the leaves; arms and legs were woven together in an intimate embrace, her golden head resting on his chest fast asleep, both naked. I glanced back to Hephaistos and saw a tear roll down his mangled cheek. I heard him sniffle.

"Oh, my dear, I am so sorry," I whispered.

"Do not be. Helios told me that they still lie together. Ares even got his servant, Alektryon, to help them keep it hidden from me, raise the alarm whenever I was nearing, and so forth," he replied gruffly.

Peering down into the trees, I could see the nymph huddling behind a bush, separated from the couple, keeping watch. But evidently, he could not see Hephaistos's view from above.

"One day soon, Alektryon will fail at his duty, and I will be able to confront them once and for all," Hephaistos continued, speaking more to himself than to me.

I shifted uncomfortably in my seat, knowing deep down that this was, in a very significant way, my fault entirely. I could have said no to his wish to marry Aphrodite. I could have kicked up a fuss and stopped the celebrations. I could have prevented Aphrodite from entering the bridal chamber as she had desperately wanted me to do. But I did not do any of those things, and now there was heartbreak.

A few days later, during one assembly of the court where Zeus was presiding and making judgement and governmental decisions, there came shouts and yells from behind the golden double doors at the back of the hall as Hephaistos burst in, dragging behind him the naked figures of Aphrodite and Ares captured, wrapped up in a long tightly-meshed golden net. Iron balls in the rope dug into their skin and bruised it. Aphrodite's hair was caught in the rope, making her cry. Ares desperately pulled at the strings around his body to rip himself free. Still, Hephaistos was no simpleton despite his appearance and his limp. Aphrodite and Ares were not leaving unless the one who had created the net of gold let them go.

The courtiers shouted in alarm as Hephaistos shoved through the gathered mob. Finally, he dumped his catch at our feet when he finally reached the dais. Ares and Aphrodite stopped struggling, realising that all eyes were on them.

I stared at them all in horror.

"Hephaistos!" Zeus shouted, jumping to his feet. "What is the meaning of this?"

"My lord Zeus. Forgive me for disturbing court matters, but I have a complaint for which I require your immediate intervention. I have suffered much in my marriage, but this ongoing humiliation by my wife, her affair with Ares, my own brother, I cannot endure."

Zeus glowered. "First, release them. They are not animals, although they evidently give in to their base instincts too often. Then we can discuss a solution."

Hephaistos shook his head. "Forgive me, Father, but I shall not. They have wronged me too much for me to simply let them go without punishment."

"I will pay any ransom you desire to free my brother," Hermes said, stepping forward.

"As will I," Apollo agreed.

"I am willing to pay the most," Poseidon said, emerging from the crowd. He had recently returned to Olympos to collect his children, Arion and Despoina, from the nursery and bring them home to his wife, Amphitrite. "I have a kingdom of my own and the greatest wealth of all the gods save for Zeus himself."

"Very well." Scowling, Hephaistos took a knife from his tool belt and cut the ropes, letting Ares and Aphrodite free themselves.

I stepped forward and took my cloak off my shoulders, wrapping it around Aphrodite's shoulders to protect what little dignity she had left.

She grabbed it and held it in place herself without any thanks.

Ignoring her, I quickly glanced at Ares. He did not look ashamed in his bare state. He stood, his feet grounded, and stared proudly at his father.

Zeus glared down at me. "Hera, escort the ladies outside. It is unbecoming for them to see this."

I glanced sideways at the harem. In no rush to leave, I slowly rounded them up.

"Have I done something wrong, my lord?" Ares demanded in the meantime.

Zeus huffed and sat back down. "It is unlawful to bed another's wife, especially that of your brother."

"Aphrodite was mine before his."

"He is your family," his father continued. "The moment Aphrodite was his, under the city's law, you should have left her alone and shown Hephaistos some respect."

Ares clenched his jaw and looked down.

"As for you," Zeus continued, looking down at Aphrodite. "What a disappointment this is that you have submitted to your desires so quickly. Have you no restraint?"

Aphrodite did not reply.

Looking at her, the rosy glow in her cheeks, and the shared glance of reassurance between her and Ares, I felt a pang of guilt.

"What are you going to do?" Hephaistos demanded.

"I am going to make this very simple," my husband replied. "Should Aphrodite ever again seek the bed of another, in such a manner as this, she shall be banished from Olympos and can go back to Kypros from whence she first came, where she can rule the matters of lust however she pleases."

At that, Aphrodite lifted her head, her mouth parted in shock. "My lord!" she gasped.

"Here on Olympos, my laws and the institution of my wife shall be respected," Zeus emphasised, giving a slight nod in my direction.

It was the first time I could remember my husband vouching for me but it was not the moment I would have picked.

"Aphrodite, you must give your word that you will be loyal to your husband or suffer exile," Zeus added, giving her a pointed look.

After a few moments of silence, she opened her mouth, her lower lip trembling, eyes shining, and said, "I, Aphrodite, shall not lie with anyone but my husband, Hephaistos."

"Or suffer exile?" Zeus pushed.

She closed her eyes, and tears slipped out from underneath her lashes. "Or suffer exile," she repeated quietly.

Ares looked at the floor with a blank expression.

"Well, good, that is settled then," Zeus said, clasping his hands.

Aphrodite spun on her heels and charged out of the throne room, tears streaming down her cheeks.

Everyone called after her for her to return. Zeus hurled a lightning bolt after her at her disobedience, but it only struck the door. A thunderous clap sounded above the sky, making the courtiers squirm and duck in fear.

Ares started after her, visible concern on his face.

Hephaistos strode after them, rage in every movement.

Zeus then glared at me, and I felt a shiver run down my spine. "Fix this, Hera. It was your cursed idea, after all," he hissed.

Nodding, I hurried after them.

After several days of searching for Aphrodite, I came to the forests of Kypros. The sunlight streamed through the crowns of the trees, showing the way created by her flighty footsteps on the soft ground. Past shrubbery and under branches, I stepped, slowly following her trail. There were several times when mud met with rock, and I lost them, having to search for them again; so, I had to go steadily and quietly, fearing she would hear me in the distance and bolt again. I doubted she thought anyone was still after her.

Being left alone with only my thoughts to entertain me, I meditated on my promise to Aphrodite's mother, Dione, to keep her daughter safe and happy and to be wary of her inclinations. I could not help feeling that I had utterly failed them both.

Had it been right to force Aphrodite to marry Hephaistos? Of course not. Would it have been disastrous had I broken my promise to my son that he could have her for his wife? Most likely so. Either way, it was bound to be tumultuous, so I had favoured my relationship with Hephaistos, but I had not expected Aphrodite's lack of restraint or consideration for the feelings of others. When I first met her, she only ever tried to spread love, but now love walked hand in hand with jealousy, hot-headedness, and rashness. Aphrodite could not be bundled into promises that her emotions dictated her to oppose. Love did what it wanted. Only the Moirai knew what I was about to get myself into now.

Approaching a clearing in the forest, I saw Aphrodite sitting on a rock in front of a stream. Birds were singing in the trees nearby. Fawns with dappled backs lay at her feet. Red squirrels diligently brought her nuts and berries, which she placed in her lap. She gazed tearfully into her hands, not at the wondrous nature around her.

I cleared my throat.

She looked up, her stern expression seeming unsurprised at my appearance. She did not even rise to her feet. "What do you want?"

I approached, struggling to remember the words I had been preparing. "I have come to bring you home."

She raised an eyebrow.

I shuffled. "Zeus has said that since your marriage was my idea, I need to fix it."

She nodded. "At least he, too, sees that you are to blame."

I could feel waves of anger radiate off her.

"What, in the name of Gaia, were you trying to achieve?" she suddenly spat. "Forcing me to wed someone I do not love, hindering my freedom? Would it have been so bad to ask me for my own wishes before choosing my husband?"

"I do not know what I was thinking, but I am so sorry." It was a pitiful response.

"Well, just try to explain yourself. Bother for once. I deserve that, at least."

"When Hephaistos told me he wanted to be your husband more than anything in the world, I had already promised him his greatest desire."

"Before you even knew what it was?" she demanded, her voice laced with disbelief.

"Yes. When my son returned to Olympos, I was so ashamed of not being there for him during his childhood. I had to make it up to him somehow."

She scoffed. "So, you bought his love with my servitude?"

I lowered my eyes. "I stupidly agreed, blind to what it would do to you."

That was when she rose to her feet. "Blind?" she hissed. "The goddess of marriage was blind to what matrimony does. How can you say that?"

"As I said, I was not in my right mind."

"You are pathetic!" she scolded, her voice harsh. "So deplorable that you must bring others down to make yourself feel superior. How can you possibly justify yourself? How can you claim your right to be here when everything you stand for does not even work? Your own union is a disaster. You are a mother to children who are not yours. Those who are, you do not love. You have tortured and killed those who have lain with your husband. You have committed crimes against them and their children. Please tell me because I struggle to understand why you even exist."

When I did not respond because I could not bring myself to, she sighed and continued: "Until you can tell me why I deny my own happiness for the rest of time, I shall be with Ares in whatever way I see fit. He is the one I love. He makes me feel loved. If there is some natural law to pick one person to be with, he is the one for me. So, I shall return to Olympos to be with him, and, if anyone has a problem with that, I shall go into exile and bring him with me. In the meantime, figure out what you stand for."

Then she moved past me, going out of the clearing.

I sat down on the rock. Aphrodite was right. It had been a question I had been avoiding for years. What was I meant for? Was I just some dreaded spirit bringing pain and anguish upon others? The idea that marriage, which I was meant to govern, promote, and encourage others to participate in, could be an evil thing saddened my soul.

Marriage could not be just the act of mixing with another; it had to be the vows and public promises. It made sense — I was the only one Zeus had publicly declared his loyalty and care for; he had not done this for his concubines. Yet some courtiers viewed his concubines and children as legitimate family members, just not royal.

I returned to Olympos with one thing on my mind: if I was doing no good, what was I doing here at all?

Aphrodite and Ares made a big show of returning to Olympos, kneeling before Zeus on his throne, begging for his forgiveness, and promising to respect the bounds of marriage for Aphrodite and Hephaistos. Zeus forgave them. Then,

Aphrodite ran into her husband's arms, kissing him fiercely and swearing to be a dutiful and faithful wife.

However, Aphrodite was never going to keep her promise. Only a few weeks later, after I knocked on the doors of Ares's suite of rooms and entered his quarters, I heard their laughter. Upon turning a corner, I saw Aphrodite sitting in sheets on his bed, with his arm draped around her shoulder. They were sharing grapes with each other. Ares was holding them up over Aphrodite's head, and her neck was tilted back as the purple berries fell into her mouth.

I watched them for a moment, seeing the smiles on their faces, particularly that of Ares. I did not often see my firstborn smile. I finally saw it. Moody was Ares's middle name. But here I saw it: in the arms of love, war could not prosper; in the arms of war, love was absent. They cancelled each other out. They were meant for each other, after all. I glanced down at the cloth in my hands, clean linen for his bed.

"Mother?" his voice said.

I looked at them. The smiles had vanished from both their faces. But while Ares gazed at me with anxious alarm, Aphrodite was scowling, eyes lowered.

"I only came to deliver these." I put the linen in a cupboard in the corner of the room.

"Did you not think to knock?" Aphrodite's sharp voice sounded.

I straightened and faced her, but still, she did not look at me. "I did. No one answered, but I have no intention of disturbing you further."

I turned away from them and headed towards the door.

"Mother?" Ares's voice called.

I stopped, hearing scuffling and quiet protests from Aphrodite.

My son appeared before me. "Would you like to stay? We were about to have dinner."

He looked at me with a warm, welcoming gaze. Dimples showed in his cheeks, and his silver eyes twinkled. At that moment, he reminded me of his father if Zeus had ever been capable of a genuine smile.

"Thank you, but I am not sure Aphrodite would like it."

He shrugged. "Well, I would like you to stay. You are my mother, after all. Is it not the duty of a loyal son to take care of his parents? Truly, I insist."

He turned around and walked away down the corridor towards the living area.

I slowly followed him, moving past the archway into his bedchamber. I glanced to the side and saw Aphrodite sitting on the bed, the sheets drawn up around her.

She looked away immediately but not before I quickly caught her glare.

I moistened my lips, feeling the need to speak. "You inspire kindness in him that I have never seen before. It is refreshing."

She did not reply.

"Aphrodite," I began, moving towards her again. I spoke quietly, not wanting Ares to overhear. "I see what I should have realised years ago: how at peace you make Ares, and how happy he makes you."

A muscle in her jaw flickered. She kept her gaze down.

"Part of me almost believes that you probably have it within your power to please both my sons. However, I am grateful for whomever you choose. You were once my closest friend. I know we may never be close again, but I hope I can make it up to you one day. If you ever want my help, I will give it without question."

Her breathing was heavy. She shook her head, seeming to scoff.

"Oh, Hera," she whispered. "If you truly support my relationship with Ares, I can forgive you. I just needed to hear it."

She reached out her arms, inviting me to take her hands. "It is not in me to hate you when I have loved you not just as a cousin or a sister but sometimes even as a mother."

We embraced in tearful relief and joy. Then, we turned to see Ares standing in the archway. Our dinner was ready, but Aphrodite's small smile showed I was finally welcome to stay. However, despite her forgiveness, Aphrodite and I were never close again. We were no longer enemies but would never be on the same side again. To lose the goddess of love, even by the slightest amount, is no small matter.

13: ATHENE

The weather was nearly always beautiful in Hellas. The sun touched every surface. Olympos's white walls glistened brighter. The fields were greener. The sky was a lovely light blue. The songbirds sang in the trees all through the day.

I was standing outside in the flower gardens, having breakfast on the terrace. I felt a grape burst in my mouth, thrilling my tastebuds, and I smiled. I was about to turn to a nearby serving girl, holding an amphora, for more mead when I heard a crashing sound coming from one of the rooms above our heads, followed by shouting. I nodded to a pair of guards nearby, ordering them to go and investigate.

I was about to retake my seat when an agonised scream flew into the air as if a soul was being tortured to its core. Everything within me told me the strangled cry belonged to my eldest daughter. So, I hurried after the guards, filled with fear and urgency. Once I arrived at Athena's bedchamber, standing in the doorway, whatever had happened was now over. The guards had kicked down the door, and bits of splintered and broken wooden planks were scattered over the marble floor. It was evident that the room had been ransacked.

Athena was sitting upright in bed, alarmed and dishevelled. Her dress was torn, her face blotchy. Gulping when she saw me, she turned away.

"Leave," I instructed the guards.

They bowed and left Athena and me alone.

I stepped into the bedchamber. "What happened? Who did this to you?"

"I am fine," she said firmly, looking at me over her shoulder as she stood up. Her eyes were wide, trying to be honest and positive. But she was far from all right. She leaned on the bedpost for support.

I approached her. "So you do not deny that someone was in here?" I pressed.

Her lower lip wobbled, and she could not look me in the face anymore.

Heart pounding, I knew it was true — she had been attacked. "Was it a god or goddess? Nymph or spirit?"

She swallowed and muttered through gritted teeth. "A god."

Coming closer, I shook my head. "Athena, you have always been strong and always will be. I imagine you gave him hell, just as anyone would expect from you."

Her shoulders began to shake. Her façade began to crumble.

"Did he succeed?"

"No," she sobbed.

"I am so proud of you. This is not your fault. You have nothing to be ashamed of. But you are wrong if you think you are protecting yourself by not telling me who did this. It is not your burden to bear. It is his. Anyone who thinks otherwise will spend eternity in the Fields of Punishment."

She looked at me again, her eyes filled with terror. Tears were already streaming down her face. "I cannot," she said.

I spied her thighs. As well as scratches, there was a faint colouring of black fingerprints on her skin, not bruises, but fingerprints of dust. *No, not dust; soot.*

At that moment, I knew who had done this, and my heart filled with dread and shame. I moved to hold Athena, to comfort and reassure her. "I shall send some maidservants in to help you clean up. If you want, you may have an armed guard escort you everywhere."

She shook her head. "No, thank you. It would only draw attention, which is the last thing I want. Besides, I fought him off once. I can do it again."

"As I said," I told her, smiling gently. "You are strong, Athena. No god could ever bring you down."

Once the nymphs came and took her away to clean up and burn her clothes, I marched through the palace halls. I found him in a conversation between two statesmen. All I could see was his smiling, flushed face. I saw scratches on his face and his dishevelled hair.

Feeling numb, I walked up to him.

He spotted me and gave me a forced smile. "Mother."

My voice was quiet. "Did you try to force yourself on Athena?"

He blinked, and I saw the flash of fear fly across his face. "No."

Nothing could have stopped me from smacking my son across the face.

Hephaistos stumbled backwards, unbalanced in shock.

The others scurried away, fearful they could be next.

"How dare you?" I said, my voice still hoarse. "I saw the soot on her thighs. I saw your fingerprints."

He steadied himself and huffed. "I wasn't planning on it. It was originally Poseidon's idea. He was angry that she won Athens instead of him. You get the rest.".

I blinked, stunned at the information and the way in which it was given. I had to laugh. "I do not care if the idea came from the great Chaos himself!" I scoffed. Finally, the anger hit. "She is your sister. How could you do that to her?"

He spluttered, trying to find the right words.

My heart was sinking. After I had confided in him about the ways in which Zeus had treated me, I had expected better. So much better. "You have no idea how disappointing and embarrassing this is," I muttered, shaking my head at him.

He faltered. "Mother, I — Aphrodite does not love me and never will, I fear."

"Neither does Athena," I muttered, feeling lower with every moment. "After this, she most certainly never will. I won't even mention what other goddesses will think."

He looked down, shoulders drooping. "I am sorry. I…"

"Tell it to her, not me," I muttered and turned away. "I don't want to hear another word on the matter from you."

I couldn't look at him. When I returned to my bedchamber, I couldn't even look at myself in the mirror. That my son, who was all mine and not a bit of Zeus, could still sink to that level, and his excuse was mindlessness and loneliness, made me feel more hopeless than anything before.

I found Athena standing on the edge of Olympos, staring out onto Hellas.

Without turning her head, she spoke: "I want to be alone."

"No, you do not," I said, coming up to her. "More than anything else, you need someone to comfort you. Well, I am here."

She glanced at me, her eyes bloodshot, her face streaked from tears. "Thank you."

I embraced her, and she sobbed fiercely into my shoulder, grasping me tightly. I noticed the white seed of Hephaistos clinging to her clothing. Disgusted, I flicked it off her robe, off the edge of Olympos. Unknown to either of us at the time, it landed on the Earth's surface, on Gaia, and from it was born Erechtheus, who became King of Athens, where he set up a statue of Athena in the Acropolis.

I looked at her. "Remember, I am your mother. You can always come to me."

She nodded and remained silent in my arms.

I dragged Hephaistos by the earlobe to Athena's chambers the following day. I made him stand in the doorway in front of her, with her blade at the ready, until he apologised.

Blushing in mortification, he did: "Athena, I wish to atone for my attack on you yesterday. It was a cowardly and shameful act born out of insecurity and fear. I had no desire to hurt you, but I did not consider the damage my actions would have caused. I am truly sorry and hope you can forgive me one day."

Athena stood there with a stony expression.

I expected her to say something to him, but she did not; she remained silent until it became apparent that he was no longer worthy of anything she had to say. Then she closed the door in his face.

Unfortunately, Hephaistos paid no more for his actions than that, which, sincere or not, was the equivalent of putting a dressing on a wound. For a long time, the damage remained raw and like it was bleeding before slowly drying up. In his stupidity, he had destroyed much.

As for Poseidon, I could never imagine even wanting to see his face again. I had just been able to bear his presence after his attack on Demeter, but to orchestrate the same upon Athena was unforgivable.

Under Zeus's reign, such crimes went unpunished. In time it became law on Earth that only a woman's guardian could bring a formal complaint against a man who raped her, not the victim herself. The thought made my heart sink. What sort of world was he building? What was I supposed to do with the women who prayed to me in those moments?

Meanwhile, Aphrodite continued to live with Ares. Their relationship became common knowledge. She had more children with him: Phobos, the god of fear; Deimos, the god of terror; Eros, the god of desire; and Anteros, the avenger of unrequited love. Yet, it was true: marriage commitments were not for them. Ares pursued the romantic and sexual attention of many more, most famously Eos, the goddess of dawn, whom Aphrodite grew particularly jealous of, and another lover called Teirene. For her part, Aphrodite also had other romantic entanglements, including with Poseidon, Hermes, and the mortal Adonis.

There was a maiden called Psyche who was renowned for her beauty, so much so that many people began to worship her instead of Aphrodite. In the goddess's rage, she sent Eros to Psyche to compel her to fall passionately in love with whoever was the most repulsive odious man alive. Instead, he fell in love with her himself. With the help of Zephyros, the god of the west wind, Psyche came to Eros's home and lay with him every night. As he went away in the morning, she never saw his face. When her sisters advised her that she may lie with a monster, Psyche resolved to kill him. One night, after her husband fell asleep, she lit a candle and took up a dagger. Still, candlelight revealed Eros as the most handsome being she had ever seen. The hot oil from the candle fell and awoke Eros, burning him. So shocked was Psyche that she stumbled back and pierced herself with one of her husband's arrows, making her enamoured with him. He fled in anger and pain when he saw her looking back at him.

Psyche tried to pursue him but could not fly like he could. Soon, she became lost. Coming to a river bank, she was discovered and aided by the god Pan. She went to her sisters for help, but they grew jealous at the realisation that her husband was a god, so they went to Zephyros to be taken in the air to the house of Eros, but when they jumped into the air to be carried away on the wind, they just fell to their deaths. Psyche roamed the earth in search of her long-lost love, coming to the temple of Demeter, but found no help there. Then she happened upon my temple in a green valley. After passing through the doors, she knelt at the altar and prayed to me:

"Lady Hera, in my dreadful and unfortunate situation, I come to you, the goddess of marriage, tired from all my difficulties and seek liberty from them by your hand, for I am with child. Yet, I cannot find my husband for help, and I know you often help those in need."

I appeared to her with a heavy heart and said: "I wish I could help you, dear child, but alas, I cannot. I would not wish to offend Aphrodite by granting shelter and safety to her enemy. Furthermore, as you were once her priestess, my husband's laws prevent me from giving refuge to another god's fleeing devotees."

I felt terrible about abandoning this young woman, in her condition, to a life of hardship. Still, I did not desire to create any further rift between myself and Aphrodite.

The goddess came to me soon after, saying: "Thank you for not getting involved with that little hussy. With no one else to turn to, she came to me for help. So, I took her in and gave her what she deserves."

"How so?"

She smirked. "I gave her several tasks. She cheated a lot, but I saw right through it. First, I told her to count and separate various seeds, but somehow, she convinced an army of ants to do it. Afterwards, I sent her to collect water from the river Styx, but she summoned an eagle to do it for her. Then I told her that if she could think to usurp me, she must retrieve some of Persephone's beauty. I did not believe she would even get to Haides's fortress, but Charon, that pestilent boatman, showed her the way. Queen Persephone, ever one to please, placed some of her beauty in a box and gave it to the mortal wretch. When I instructed Psyche to open the box, having breathed the scent of the Queen of the Dead, she fell ill. Now she lies sick at my temple. No one shall worship her now."

"Does Eros know of his wife's state?" I asked, feeling sympathy for the poor girl.

"It will be nothing compared to the heartbreak she has already inflicted on him."

After hearing this, I told Eros of Psyche's plight. Grief-stricken, he fetched Psyche and came before the court to petition Zeus to intercede. "My lord, I cannot be without her."

After seeing how the courtiers had fallen for the love story, Zeus conceded: "I know. Your mother may be the goddess of love, but she is certainly not the goddess of fidelity. Perhaps this will show her how to behave," Zeus said, glowering at Aphrodite, at his side. "Psyche is welcome on Olympos. I shall make her a goddess, perhaps that of the soul, and you shall have your wedding with Hera presiding."

Aphrodite sat there, furious and wholly ignorant of my part in it.

The wedding of Eros and Psyche was as grand and legendary as the rest before it, its splendour bettered only by my wedding festivities long ago. I am also happy that Eros and Psyche lived happily ever after, one of the few married couples worldwide to remain happy together. It almost felt like proof of what I believed was possible.

In a surprising announcement given by Ares to the court of Olympians, Aphrodite gave birth to a child of Hermes, with whom she had been in an affair recently. They would name the new godling Hermaphroditos. I spoke to Ares about the nature of his relationship with her.

"How are you feeling?" I asked him as I emerged from Aphrodite's bedchamber to the living area, where he was drinking mead to relieve his nerves.

"What do you mean?"

I shrugged. "It is not every day that your lover gives birth to another's child."

He took a sip of mead from his goblet. "You prefer monogamy, Mother. That is perfectly understandable. Such loyalty requires much strength. However, Aphrodite and I are happier when we are free to be with others. It makes us appreciate each other more. We are open to learning more about ourselves, first and foremost."

"I admire your ability to not feel any jealousy."

He chuckled. "Oh, I feel jealousy. So does she. I return to her if there is someone she is jealous of, and she does the same for me. The essential ingredient is honesty."

I did not doubt Aphrodite and Ares's devotion to each other. Still, I could not see it as a proper marriage, as they had never had a ceremony. While I admired the arrangement in principle, I imagined it only caused more hurt in practice.

I wondered in that moment if Aphrodite had taught me more than anyone. She had forced me to consider the meaning and purpose of marriage and, thus, of myself. She made me face the circumstances of my role as a goddess of matrimony and motherhood, as well as the differences between love, lust, and loyalty, and how none or all or some of them are in a marriage. However, I could not find a solid reason why what I stood for was necessary. At the same time, as I looked upon Eros and Psyche, I could not think of a single thing that made me more impassioned than the ideal family, a family which I did not have. So then, what kind of goddess of marriage and motherhood was I?

As for Hephaistos, it was a relief when he apologised to Athena. He seemed genuine in his remorse, so I found it easier to forgive him. As for Aphrodite, I do not believe he stopped loving her, but he requested Zeus return his dowry: a divorce. Zeus reluctantly agreed to this, most likely keen to put the scandalised marriage he had ordered in the past.

I, too, found it hard to accept initially. However, in time I came to appreciate that divorce might make more sense than a marriage without desire or with a partner unable to honour the marriage vows. However, then dowries had to be returned. Children stayed with the father since he owned them, leaving the mother distraught, returning to her own father or brother for care, or in some extreme cases, homeless and without any support. I had great pity for divorced women who were suddenly treated as outcasts. If their marriage had failed, they were unfit for contribution to society and of no further value.

Hephaistos found happiness in a relationship with Aglaia, one of the three Charites, the goddess of magnificence and splendour. With her, he had four daughters: Eukleia, the goddess of glory; Euthenia, the goddess of prosperity; Eupheme, the goddess of praise; and Philophrosyne, the goddess of friendliness and kindness. Seeing the joy he had finally found in his life was beautiful, one of the few comforts I took from the mess I had created.

Athena came to Asklepios, the god of medicine, with me in tow. Since the day Hephaistos had attacked her, I had a slight idea of what she was planning but nothing definite, considering the last several days and our conversations about them.

We arrived at his temple in Hellas. Walking past the columns, we came to a green sanctuary where all his patients strolled — some hobbled, some in anguish — between the dining and resting areas. Many were clearly suffering from physical or cognitive defects or injuries. I felt uncomfortable, but I did not know why. Perhaps it was because I was unfamiliar with what ailed them. Maybe it was because I felt useless. I glanced sideways at Athena. She did not seem discomforted by any of it. As was common practice, I would have had our divine physician come to Mount Olympos. Still, she had insisted on coming here to avoid drawing attention to the matter back at home.

We reached the back of the temple, two large golden doors, each with an enormous engraving of a snake wrapped around a staff — the sceptre of Asklepios.

"Are you sure about this?" I whispered to Athena.

"This is what I need," she said. Then she looked at me. "I am sorry, Mother. I know how this must disappoint you."

"On the contrary, my dear. I want you to be happy." I wore a supportive smile, although it was a lie. The idea that she wanted to relinquish her femininity hurt everything I stood for.

"Are you nervous?" I asked.

"Yes," she whispered.

I reached forward and squeezed her hand gently. "If it does not go well, we shall figure something else out."

She nodded, letting out a shaky breath.

The doors opened, and we stepped inside a small atrium where various recliners were gathered around a small table laden with platters of fruits and cold meats. We sat down, and in time, Asklepios joined us. He was the Hellenic epitome of the wise old man with kind, lined eyes and a thick, curly white beard.

"It is a great honour to receive a visit from some of the highest in the land," he said, chuckling slightly. He walked into the room, leaning on his staff. He stood before us, bowed his head, and sat opposite us.

I smiled. "We understand you are a very busy doctor."

"Indeed, but I will always make time for Olympian patients." He glanced between us. "Now, as you are both so radiant, forgive me if I enquire as to whom I am to treat."

After a quick glance at each other, Athena spoke up. "Me."

He smiled pleasantly. "What can I do for you, my lady?"

"It is not easy to describe. I doubt it will be easy to treat."

He did not comment, waiting for her to find the right words.

"Since I was born, I have always been deemed the son my father never had," Athena began nervously. "I suppose I have found myself identifying more and more with that. I have always related more to my brothers. I have always felt uncomfortable in female circles, like I did not belong. I have never liked the look of my body. I made efforts to be more muscular. When I was younger, I took a blade to my breasts to have a man's chest. I have always tried to appear more masculine. I suppose that is my point."

Asklepios nodded along with her words, humming thoughtfully. He was taking the news much better than I ever had. "Yes, some females prefer to be male to live happier lives."

Athena closed her eyes before taking a deep breath. "It is more than that for me. It feels like I am trapped, stuck in the wrong body."

Asklepios did not respond.

"I suppose I am not making any sense," she sighed, looking down and blushing.

"I will confess I have never had someone describe their ailments as relating to their gender, although I have had plenty of people struggle with their identities. Some believe many different people are living inside them. Some struggle to understand social normalities —"

"I am not mad!" Athena snapped. "There is nothing wrong with me."

He smiled kindly. "Forgive me, my lady, but mad people would naturally refuse to believe they were mad. No. I would go so far as to say that everyone carries some burden of the soul, which can differ from what most believe is normal. Nevertheless, being different can be excellent. Different is special. It is unique. It is wondered at or reviled by those who fear it."

Athena's initial annoyance seemed to ebb. "What are you saying?"

"I am saying that identity issues come in all shapes and sizes. There are very few who are genuinely content in this world. Almost everyone has a problem with who they are. Even the man who has everything feels dissatisfied with who he is and what he has in his life. There is nothing uncommon about that. However, some issues go undiscussed because they are harder to explain, problems such as your own. When it comes to identity, almost anything is possible. It is my endeavour to help you find peace in yourself by whatever means I can."

My heart seemed to feel lighter and heavier at the same time while I listened to his words. Although Asklepios was addressing Athena on a particular issue, I felt he was also talking to me. *When it comes to identity, almost anything is possible.*

Her shoulders relaxed slightly. "I see," she mumbled.

"We must identify the best course of action for you, personally. Everyone has different needs and requirements when it comes to treatment. I will speak with you privately, and we can explore those options together," Asklepios suggested.

Athena nodded, a hopeful smile edging its way onto her face.

"After that, I would like you to return home. Take some time to consider if there is anything your family, other than Queen Hera," he smiled at me, "can do to help you. Speak to those you trust. They say that a problem shared is a problem halved. Try to find those who may have had similar struggles to you."

She frowned. "I doubt there are any."

"You have a cousin, I believe, called Hermaphroditos, a creature of both sexes, a male god and a female nymph melded together for eternity. Why not share your concerns with them? See if they can help," he suggested.

Athena nodded. "Very well, doctor. I shall do as you suggest."

Then he turned to me. "My queen, is there anything I can do for you?"

Momentarily, I considered it. It seemed tempting, yet my heart sank at the realisation that even the best physician could prescribe no remedy for my situation. So, I shook my head.

Upon returning to Olympos, we sought out Hermaphroditos, a deity with female curves, shoulder-length wavy hair and feminine facial features, bearing a prim nose and wide eyes with long lashes and dimples. They also had long, shaped nails and flowers in their hair. But for all of that, they had male genitals. We found them reclining in a woodland spring in the forests outside Olympos on the mountainside, resting amid birdsong in the shade of the trees.

They looked up as we approached, treading on twigs and dry leaves. "My lady Hera. My lady Athena," they greeted. "How may I help you?"

Athena explained her predicament and was met with applause and smiles at her journey of self-discovery. Then Hermaphroditos invited her into the water.

I sat away from them, in disbelief that such a conversation was happening several feet away from me. It seemed hardly normal in polite society. It made me blush.

Athena emerged from the water, bright-eyed. "They have everything," she gasped to me.

Hermaphroditos chuckled at her awed tone and surprised facial expression and said, "Our labels only live in our minds, and we dictate each other according to them with little room for change. But none of us can live that way, assigned to a word and remain so forever. What label would you give me?"

She shrugged. "I have not the slightest idea."

Hermaphroditos smiled. "Me neither, if I'm being perfectly honest, but I have come to think it is for the best."

Those words inspired Athena greatly. She entered a newfound place of delight and hope like I had never seen in her before. Upon her return to the physician Asklepios, she requested that he remove her womb and close her birth canal, which he did. He invited her to stay at his temple weeks before and after the operation. The surgery was a success. Afterwards, Asklepios provided Athena with potions to make her body hair grow. She kept her hair cut close to the scalp. Then she emerged from the treatment chambers at the sanctuary of Asklepios, beaming from ear to ear, where I was waiting for her.

"Well?" Athena said, spinning in front of me.

I gazed down at the straightness of her body, the slight dip at her waist and the lean muscles on her arms, her hair cut short. The truth was that she did not look much different. She had more hair on her arms and some wisps on her chin, but her face was the same, with her grey eyes. It seemed so strange to me. However, while I did not know what to make of it, I knew Athena was no longer what she had once been. She was as near to the version of herself she had always wanted to be: as unfeminine as possible.

"I think you look great," I said. "Are you happy?"

Athena nodded energetically. "I have even thought of a new name."

"Really? The final touch?" I chuckled.

"I shall call myself Athene. Athen-ah is simply too feminine."

I smiled. "Athene it is."

She blushed slightly before saying: "Furthermore, I would also rather be referred to as 'they' and 'them' rather than 'she' and 'her'."

That confused me slightly, but I did not question it. "As you wish, my dear."

Athene came forward and hugged me tightly. "Thank you so much for being here."

I wrapped my arms around them. "Of course," I whispered into their head.

Athene returned to Olympos and lived happily thereafter. Or as much as that was possible. Athene, with the being they had become and the changes they had made, was no longer disguised by a feminine body and face. They were visible now and could not go ignored or unnoticed. To any who were confused or who challenged them, Athene let it be known they were no longer god nor goddess but the entity of wisdom and enlightenment for all.

14: DIONYSOS

History is seldom kind, even to gods. The annals never forget what each individual did despite the passing millennia. The past often reappears before us in the strangest of ways and in various forms and figures. Sometimes one does not always see at first the memories that have come to life around oneself. Sometimes, they are unmistakable.

That is why, when Dionysos returned to Olympos, I was only one of a handful who instantly recognised him. Others included his father and his older siblings. None had forgotten the day he burst forth from his father's thigh. Some had vague memories of when he shared their nursery before Hermes had stolen him away from Olympos and given him to Rhea for safekeeping.

When Zeus called the next court assembly, everyone gathered in the throne room, lining up against the walls, eagerly awaiting us.

Among the sea of faces I took in as I entered on Zeus's arm, all of whom I was familiar with, one individual stood before the dais, who turned around at the sound of our approach.

I nearly stopped short when I saw him, immediately knowing who he was.

Dionysos had grown tall, lean and muscular. He was dressed in a short tunic, a travel cloak draped over his shoulders, and had an amphora at his feet. His blond hair was slightly darker than his siblings, but his silver eyes flashed with excitement when he looked back at us. I felt Dionysos's eyes follow me as I passed him by and sat down on my throne.

Zeus paused when he saw his son but quickly continued walking past him. He closed his eyes for a moment and then opened them. He cleared his throat and took a deep breath.

I frowned. It was the first time I had seen something akin to weariness on Zeus's face. Usually, my husband's face brightened at the sight of everyone staring up at him, waiting for him to speak; usually, such a spectacle made his arrogance and ego soar. However, this time, he looked strained. It was a confusing sight and not comforting.

"Fair Olympians," he began. "Thank you for gathering here today so we may press on with the governance of this universe. So," he said, turning his attention to our visitor, "present yourself before the court."

Dionysos grabbed his amphora off the ground and stepped forward, looking at me and Zeus, his gaze shifting between us.

Trying to fight my blushes, my racing heart, and my sweaty palms, I realised I was facing shame: I had sent Semele, his mother, to her death and then failed to raise him as my own.

"Greetings, Lord Zeus, my heavenly father," Dionysos spoke.

His accent was strange to my ears, like it came from far beyond Hellas.

"Lady Hera, my glorious queen," he added, nodding at me. "I once lived here in these great halls under your care, but the Moirai destined me to leave this heavenly paradise and be raised by my grandmother, Rhea, and to walk among the earth's mortals for my childhood lessons. They did not disappoint. I have travelled far and wide, seeing how they live and worship the Olympian gods as Zeus decreed they would, witnessing their suffering and joy, and bringing my presence to the humans for their comfort and relief. In this, some have doubted my claim as an Olympian, so I have come home to assume my rightful place in your halls, Lord Zeus."

He then flashed a cheeky smile with dimples on his cheeks. "However, I do not come empty-handed. On my extensive travels, I made a significant discovery which I found very popular among the many with whom I shared it."

He held up his amphora. "Wine."

I frowned at the jug. *What? Whine?*

"A mixture of juices from grapes which makes one feel warm and relaxed. One finds oneself dizzy with laughter and merriment, prone to happiness. Taken with music and dance, it can be very liberating. I encourage you both to take a sip from this amphora."

He presented the jug to Zeus, who took it and regarded the contents suspiciously before sniffing it. Seeming, at first, offended by the smell, Zeus then proceeded to sip it slowly. He frowned at the taste but then took another sip and another, his face relaxing the more he drank. Then he handed the amphora to me.

"It is delicious," he proclaimed, and the hall erupted in claps.

Staring into the amphora, I saw dark purplish-red liquid. The odour was strong, and I nearly gagged on it, but it had a sweet scent at the same time. Cautiously, I raised the rim of the amphora to my lips and tasted the wine, as Dionysos called it. It was lovely and thick, lingering on my tongue. Such a strange drink: at first bitter but then a honied aftertaste, with my mouth watering for more. So, I obliged myself to take another sip. It was delicious. Soon my belly began to warm. My head felt slightly woozy. I had to lean my chin on my hand to steady my vision, but it was not unpleasant.

Not long after, all the Olympians were eager to taste this wonderous new drink.

Zeus addressed Dionysos, "How did you say it is made?"

The youth smiled. "By squeezing the juice from grapes."

The King of Heaven nodded, impressed. "Such a simple invention yet so ingenious. When can we have more of it?"

Dionysos grinned. "I can make it for you whenever you like and would be happy to teach the servants of this palace my methods."

Zeus thought for a moment. "I do not see why not. Progress must not be hindered by anything," he declared.

With that, Dionysos had made the most triumphant homecoming yet.

"What do you think of him?" Maia asked me, back in my bedchamber. She was helping the nymphs draw me a bath.

I shook my head, lifting my arms up so the nymphs could unpin my dress. "I am not sure. He was still an infant when he left my care. However, my mother, Rhea, will undoubtedly have doted on him as the only child she could ever raise. I am sure she did well, being a mother goddess herself."

"Naturally, he should seem somewhat wild and uncivilised, I suppose. Barbaric even." She hummed. "Maybe it was just his appearance. He did look quite rugged."

I ruffled my hair, sore after the day of plaits and twists. "A life of travel, mixing with different cultures, can do that, I suppose."

She hesitated before asking: "Do you think he will get on with his siblings?"

"You are very curious, Maia."

"My lady, I only think of the effect his worldly knowledge will have on my Hermes."

Indeed, Dionysos had many stories to tell, which he relayed to the court at his own welcome feast. I was not surprised when he showed he was his father's son, constantly bragging about his exciting life. He told of how he had wandered beyond Anatolia as far as the Indus land, where he founded a city called Nysa. The only places he had not reached were Aethiopia in the south, the far-off lands of Albion and Iouernia in the west, and the ice-covered caps of Scandza in the far north.

He returned to Hellas, where he made many efforts to spread knowledge of his presence as a god and not as some would have him as a wandering magician. Many opposed him, the most famous being Prince Pentheus of Thebes, whose mother, Agave, was sister to Semele, making Prince Pentheus the first cousin of Dionysos. Since the royal family did not believe him to be a god, Dionysos caused the city's women to go into a frenzy where they could not tell friends from foes. He called them to the forests of Mount Kithaeron, where they performed rituals of madness in his honour, which, from the rumours, consisted of disgusting dances with phalli and eating live animals in his honour. This alarmed the men of the realm that their wives, daughters, and sisters had disappeared and were out of their sight and control. Pentheus, in his anguish, went searching with a retinue and came to a clearing in the woods where he saw his mother, Agave, and other women going wild among the trees. They stayed to spy on the women to see if they could catch acts of any sexual nature. Caught hiding in a tree as punishment for his impiety against Dionysos, the god cursed Pentheus to be killed by his mother's hand. Not recognising her son and believing he was a lion, she led an ambush with her fellow women, including his aunts. They attacked and killed him, ripping his head and limbs off. Only after Dionysos had let the women return to the city did they realise what had happened. Dionysos revealed himself in his proper divine form. They banished Agave and her sisters, turning Kadmos, his own grandfather, the father of Semele, and his grandmother, Harmonia, into serpents.

Next was Lykourgos, King of Thrake, who also did not believe Dionysos was a god and imprisoned his followers. Dionysos took refuge with Thetis for a while, which I was not pleased to hear. Dionysos sent a drought to Thrake. The people revolted against their king. Then Dionysos drove the king insane. In his madness, he attacked a large ivy plant sacred to Dionysos, believing it to be his son, pruning and slicing it up into pieces, leaf by leaf and branch by branch. When an Oracle decreed that the drought would remain as long as Lykourgus was king, the Thrakian people removed his innards and chopped him up until he bled to death.

Dionysos then recounted to the court how a ship passed by when he was sitting on the shoreline. The sailors believed him to be a prince and kidnapped him, hoping to profit from him through ransom or selling him as a slave. However, Dionysos would not be held and turned into a great lion, destroying them. A similar event happened on a pirate ship to the island of Naxos, where those on board tried to sail instead to Anatolia to sell him as a slave. However, the ropes and oars became snakes that attacked the sailors, and the ship was filled with ivy and flute music. In their madness, the sailors jumped into the sea, where he turned them into dolphins.

The new god's adventures took him to the rescue of his old master Silenos, a satyr, who came to the house of King Midas, where he was feted for ten days and ten nights. In a show of gratitude for Midas's kindness towards Silenos, Dionysos rewarded the king with any blessing he wanted. Midas, in his greed, sought to have anything he touched turn to gold. At first, delighted with his newfound wealth, Midas was quickly horrified to realise that he had cursed himself for he could not even drink or eat. In his starvation, he prayed to Dionysos, who showed him how to wash away the spell.

Everyone at court loved him, fascinated at how well-travelled, informed, educated, and interesting Dionysos was. No one could claim to have had as many adventures or met so many people. Those who took an interest in his stories wondered how inspiring it was that he had been victorious in the face of so many adversities and how no one else could claim to have suffered as much as he had. Not long after telling these stories, Dionysos gained many admirers and followers beyond. Those who worshipped him became known as the Maenades, known for their wild hysterical state when lauding and praising him, retreating into nature, becoming drunk on wine, dancing, sacrificing without due process, and leaving the law behind.

I was surprised that Zeus tolerated his customs so well when they went against nearly every expectation people were supposed to have of life and each other, but Dionysos had charm and charisma. He was wild and unpredictable. Festivities on Olympos used to be strictly ordered affairs, gatherings where everyone danced in carefully choreographed sequences to the Muses' band playing lively songs that kept the steps in time, with only mead to drink. He was popular. Everyone found his allure as intoxicating as the wine he served.

Everyone but me. I may not have seen as much of the mortal world as Dionysos. However, I considered that I, too, had suffered much, achieved much, and had given much to the world. I figured that I deserved friends, love, and adoration, as much as he. Yet, it was as if he had enchanted them all with his novelty. I was humdrum, while he was intriguing. I was one of the few, if not the only one, who did not hold him in any high regard, but I knew my feelings were the result of envy. I thought of him as having everything I wanted. He had an unbridled enthusiasm for life; moreover, he was allowed to. He was not expected to watch his tongue or control himself or ask permission for all he did. He had a freedom I could only dream of. Of course, he was encouraged to dance and drink as it gave everyone a sense of relief that life was not all serious. On the other hand, I was controlled, constantly told what to do and who to be. I was expected to be restrained, an example of modesty, manners, and fidelity to all. However, it was exhausting. I surmised there was no benefit in showing my feelings. So, I hid them as usual.

Then Dionysos introduced the *party*. He hosted gatherings in his quarters, serving wine and food. He preferred the sounds of drums to the high-pitched flutes of the Muses. Then as the guests drank more and more wine, their inhibitions disappeared. At first, they would start to move and writhe to the beat of the drums, but then they would grab sticks, known as the thyrsos, and bang them on the floor in time with the drums. They stripped their clothes off, becoming frenetic, waving and shaking their limbs in whatever way the whim took them as their naked bodies grew hot and sweaty. Then they put on animal skins. The wine encouraged loud groaning and roaring, chants of no consequence. All this they did until they collapsed, vomiting and exhausted on the floor. However, this did not deter them from returning the next evening.

Zeus gave in to his curiosity, and we attended one such event together. On arrival, no one heard us knocking on the door. Following decorum, we waited until my husband grew impatient and pushed through. The room was dark, dimly lit with candlelight. The air was hot and pungent, heavy with the stench of wine, sweat and meat. The drums and the pounding of thyrsos were thunderous. Crowds of naked bodies were slipping and sliding among each other in such a debauched state they were ignorant that their king and queen had just arrived. Everyone had opened their mouths, making whatever sounds their spirit called.

I saw many people locked in tight embraces. Some were having sex on the couches — many were of the same sex. I found the whole thing suffocating, dangerous, and disgusting. It seemed guests came, lost all self-control, and did what they wanted until they could do no more. As I saw it, Dionysos threatened the stability of the social order, especially the security and sanctity of matrimony and purity, and, in my mind, that had to be stopped; *he* had to be stopped.

15: ARIADNE

The only way I knew to put a check on Dionysos's behaviour was through marriage. Yes, I know I had forced Aphrodite to marry Hephaistos, this time my reasons were different — Dionysus and his new ways were dangerous. So, I went to Zeus since I needed his permission for such an event.

"I have been thinking," I said, sitting next to him at breakfast, "about Dionysos's welfare, his parties and his drinking. I wonder if he should have a wife, someone to take care of him, keep an eye on him, curb his excesses, and temper his wildness. I only ask that you think about it, my lord."

"I do not need to think about it. It is a wise idea. Dionysos should be married."

I cheered inside.

Later that day, Dionysos was summoned to a council chamber where he found Zeus and me awaiting him. He slumped into the room, sluggish and slow, and flopped himself down into a chair, holding his head in his hands. Then, looking up at us, he raised an eyebrow and said, "Well?"

"Are you feeling out of sorts, Dionysos?" I asked him.

He closed his eyes and sighed. "A mere headache, but nothing to worry about. Now, how can I be of service?" He asked, looking between us impatiently.

Zeus gave him a benevolent smile. "You came to my court to assume your rightful place among my family. However, it seems you have little idea of what that entails, the behaviour and duties expected of you. Since you choose to spend your time in a daze, unable to contribute to the world around you, I can hardly expect you to take your new position seriously. So,

Queen Hera suggested a possible solution to the problem at hand. She is the authority on the matter, and I strongly agree that it would be best if you were to marry."

Dionysos's face went slack. "You are not serious."

"I most certainly am," Zeus assured him. "If you were to take a wife, she could take care of any children you might have, clean up after your parties, and remind you of what is important. Perhaps Queen Hera could arrange it."

Dionysos stared at me. "This was your idea?"

I nodded. "No need to thank me."

He put his head in his hands. "This must be some kind of awful nightmare."

He sat there for some moments, contemplating. Then, looking determined, he said, "Very well. I shall agree to marry if I get to choose my own wife."

"An interesting proposition, Dionysos, but Hera is an expert. Let her select the perfect bride for you," Zeus said, gesturing to me. "You can trust her to make the right choice."

"Was it the right choice to pair Aphrodite and Hephaistos together?" he demanded.

"Watch yourself," Zeus growled. "I gave that betrothal my approval too."

"Let him recommend a bride," I said to Zeus. "If I approve, we will seek your final seal."

Zeus tapped his fingertips on the tabletop before saying: "Fine. However, I will not have this be a long, dragged-out process. I want a suitable candidate by tomorrow evening."

Not unexpectedly, Dionysos made my job very hard. He rejected my daughters, Hebe and Eileithyia, as possible brides; he found a problem with each of them. Then, he would not even hear of a union with any of the maidens at court. He soon tossed out each name on my list of options and presented me with his own list.

I stared at it. "They are almost entirely mortal women."

"All royals, though."

"Zeus will not allow you to marry beneath your station."

"You do not know that."

"The past would say differently."

"This is my marriage we are discussing, and Father agreed to me choosing my bride."

"Except that she must first be approved by me before he even considers letting an outsider join the Olympian family."

Dionysos huffed and clasped his hands pleadingly. "Hera, I grew up on Earth. I am familiar with its inhabitants. I enjoy the company of mortals. I find them amusing and delightful. I would wager you have barely spent a day with one."

I pursed my lips, letting him go on.

He pointed to the first name on the list. "She is my favourite one."

It was Ariadne, princess of the Kingdom of Krete. We descended to Earth to look at her. I made it a quick affair as I did not want to spend too much time with him. Holding his hand, we flew to the island of Naxos, where she had been stranded.

Indeed, a young, frail woman stood in the sea foam on the shoreline; the hem of her dress was soaked. I could see her bare legs. Her dark hair was billowing in the breeze like a flag. She was crying. Her fingers were splayed, her hands raised aloft to the sky, and her face contorted with anger and misery. Her cheeks streamed with tears as she put a hand to her chest and called out, "Theseus! Theseus, return to me!"

"Who is Theseus?" I demanded.

"The scoundrel who took her from her homeland after promising to marry her. They call him a hero because he slew the Minotaur and saved fourteen youths from being eaten alive in the Minoan labyrinth. However, he used her help abominably. He has abandoned her here. She does not deserve to die in such shame and loneliness."

I shook my head. "She might have given him her maidenhead."

"So?"

"So, she might already be pregnant!"

"Well, make your expert assessment of her then."

I took in the maiden. She was barely a woman, so naive and innocent looking. Yet her womb had been untouched, that much I could tell. "She is not with child."

"Of course not," Dionysos agreed. "They only left Krete a few days ago. They did not have the privacy or energy to consummate anything, for they all had to sleep on the beach."

"However, what does it say about her character that she willingly ran away from home?"

"It says that she was naive but has now learned better. Just look at how much she regrets her decision." Dionysos gestured to her.

"Theseus may yet come back." I genuinely feared Dionysos had not thought through the wisdom of his choice. "It all seems very hasty to me."

"He would have returned by now. Will you forsake her? My lady, you are the goddess of all women, not just mothers and wives. She was to be a bride. Look at her."

I sighed as Ariadne dropped to her knees, sobbing into her hands. "I fear she is still very much wounded from her treatment at the hands of Theseus. What happened?"

It seemed to me that Dionysos was genuine in his desire to help this maiden. The sound of her wails carried on the wind to my ears and tugged at my heartstrings.

"Very well. If Zeus approves, I hope you are happy with her," I gave in.

Ariadne was a sweet little thing — Zeus saw that, although he was shocked at the depth to which Dionysos was willing to sink below his station. Still, he reckoned, it was better than risking another drama like Aphrodite and Hephaistos, who had been well-matched in their positions.

So it was that once I had given my word that Ariadne's virginity remained intact, Dionysos was free to wed her. He brought her dead soul to Olympos.

It was an occasion with little pomp, grandeur, and a lot of wine and drums, as was Dionysos's style. However, Ariadne was relatively quiet on the morning of her wedding day. I think she put on a brave smile for the world to see. I doubted she was thrilled with her marriage and how the groom had turned out. She was also in a strange place, perhaps overwhelmed by living in Heaven. To make matters worse, true to Dionysos's unconventional way, he insisted on not having their union consummated in a bedchamber but rather on a mountainside amid nature where he was happiest. Poor Ariadne was hauled up Mount Drios that night amid gorse and stones. It must have been very uncomfortable.

I pitied Ariadne greatly, so I made it my duty to assist her in settling in. I helped her learn to do chores, prepare food for her husband, and be an Olympian wife. I often scolded Dionysos on her behalf since she was too small and weak for him to take her seriously. Unfortunately, he did not seem to consider that every time he threw a party, she could not sleep, mortified or terrified by what was happening elsewhere in their quarters. She locked herself in an antechamber until it was all over. Then, when she came out, as the sun rose in the sky at dawn, she would have to evict the stragglers and clean up the mess left behind.

One morning, I saw her in the middle of a chaotic mess in her husband's chambers, sitting on the floor, her knees curled up to her chest, shaking her head as if in wonder.

"My dear," I sighed. "What troubles you now?" I sat down next to her and put an arm around her. "It cannot be so hopeless, can it?"

"I cannot go on like this," she muttered. "I am surrounded by animals and perverts. Every night, there is a wild orgy, and I am greeted by chaos every morning. Every day, I scrape and bustle over the food they do not eat and the mess they do not care to help clean up. Dionysos is always too drunk to talk to or lie with me — he has not lain with me since our wedding night. At the same time, I must retain some strength to keep my sanity and somehow find time to enjoy myself. I cannot keep going like this."

I hugged her close. "I will speak to Dionysos. He may not have the best habits, but he is not cruel. He chose you himself, you know. He would have no other. He may not be who you wanted, but he is far more than Theseus ever was or can be. Surely being with him is a far better solution than pining on a beach for one who has betrayed you. However, you must inform him of your plight if he makes you unhappy."

She drew away from me. "I would, my lady. But he is often too drunk to understand any reason."

I frowned. Perhaps it had been a tall order to expect this mortal girl with no worldly experience to tame the wild god that was Dionysos.

She bowed her head. "Thank you, my lady. I would most appreciate it."

16: ERIS

That evening, I stood outside Dionysos's quarters. Yet I had no idea what to say to him about his wife's unhappiness: how would such a conversation go? How would he react? Dionysos was a wild and untrustworthy creature raised in the barbaric world of mortals. He was unpredictable.

Then I heard the music coming from the other side of the door. When I raised my fist to knock on it, it simply creaked open to reveal the world of hysteria Dionysos often had on the other side. The sweet scents of wine and mead seeped into my nose and mouth. My nervous heartbeat steadied to beat in time with the heavy drums. The music of the panpipes filled my ears, and while before, I had been offended by the sound, this time it spoke to me and told me to dance.

I found myself stepping inside and among the revellers, either naked or dressed in various guises of nature, some donning furs and antlers, with ivy around their necks, beating great thyrsos on the ground. My body began to sway in time to the flutes and drums. So lost were they in the melody and the rhythm they did not notice me join their throng of sweaty bodies.

I was grateful to blend in, for once, and to get lost. It was a rare opportunity. So, I took off my sandals and shawl, letting my hair loose from its brooch, and I did not refrain from dancing. I discovered a release from the tension and the anxiety. I then realised why these parties were so popular: those present just wanted to escape their stress and daily monotony.

I poured myself a fresh goblet of wine from a large amphora, the nymphs being too drunk to attend to their duties properly, and sipped at it, letting the warm, earthy yet sugary taste slip down and warm me up. Then I sipped from it again and again. It was effortless. As I moved and drank, I did not want to stop. It was a nice feeling.

Opening my eyes briefly, I saw Dionysos in front of me. I almost jumped but was too relaxed to be taken so off-guard.

He was wearing antlers tonight. Grinning, he shouted at me over loud drums, lyres, and flutes: "Are you sure you should be here without Zeus?"

I shrugged. "It has been too long."

He raised an eyebrow. "Will the king not be angry?"

"And if he is? What is the worst he could do?"

"Smite you into smithereens and chuck the rest into Tartaros."

I giggled, feeling giddy from the beat pumping through my body and the warm feeling in my chest. "Who will tell Zeus?"

He shook his head. "Not me." He looked over his shoulder. "Judging from the state of this lot, I can guarantee you that no one else here will even remember you came."

I smiled and took another sip of wine. "Then you better show me how to dance."

Together, we had a wild moment of fun. He spun me around and kept me steady on my feet as I descended into the pit of drunken forgetful dizziness. I knew there was something I was supposed to tell him, but I forgot why I had gone there.

Once everyone began to pass out, including the band musicians, I realised that I too was feeling ill on the wine and dizzy from the dancing. And so, Dionysos escorted me back to my bedchamber, where Zeus was waiting for me.

I registered my husband's enormous frame sitting on the end of the bed, just as powerful and imposing as he ever had been. Fear might have filled me on an average day, but this time I felt too sick to be scared.

"Father," Dionysos gasped. "What are you doing here?"

"Waiting on my wife," Zeus replied. "What are you doing here?"

"Bringing her back to her rooms." Dionysos let me go.

I staggered towards one of the lounge chairs, stumbling.

"Did she go to one of your parties?"

"Yes, sir."

"Was she drinking?"

Dionysos was silent for a moment. Then: "Yes, my lord."

"And you did not stop it?" Zeus roared.

Another silence.

"No, my lord."

Zeus moved so quickly that even Dionysos could not have avoided the mighty strike to his face. He was thrown back, staggering, his hands rising to protect himself from another attack. He regained his footing. He stared at his father in shock.

"Oh gosh," I muttered under my breath. I was not getting a good feeling in my stomach, and my head was pounding.

"Now, I do not have very high expectations for our female companions to be able to resist certain temptations in life. Your wine creation is certainly one of them. While it is an ingenious invention, I specifically ruled against goddesses and women drinking it. From now on, for mortals, the penalty will be death," Zeus said.

Dionysos spluttered, about to interject.

Zeus continued: "I see now there is cause to ban goddesses and mortal women altogether from attending all parties where wine is consumed. Now, leave us."

Darting me a glance of warning, Dionysos scampered from the room.

I tried to stand up to face Zeus, but my legs were shaky, and my vision was hazy.

"Hera," he said, as he approached me. "Did you drink the wine yourself, or did Dionysos invite you to drink it?"

I steadied myself, thinking hard. I could not put Dionysos in the line of fire, but if I admitted to it, Zeus would beat me. That much I knew.

"I do not remember. My lord, I do not feel well." I tried to get some pity from him.

"Because you are drunk. Admit it."

"I do not know what that feels like, my lord."

He gestured to me. "Look at yourself. You are drunk!"

I gulped down some bile. I really was not feeling well.

His voice rose to a shout. "How am I supposed to know you have not been with someone else? At least when you are sober, I can somewhat rely on your common sense. Yet, without that, what else is there? Others will take advantage, Hera. Do you not know that?"

He rubbed his face with his fingertips. "Well, there is one thing I can do."

Zeus's fist flew out and drove hard and fast straight into my lower abdomen.

It was like a bull had hit me with its whole body. I stumbled back against the wall, doubling over. The shock was monumental. Once I regained some sense of the world, I glanced back up at him in surprise.

"Whatever might have been growing inside you is surely dead now," he commented, wiping his hands.

Then he took me where I stood. It was a messy and ridiculous affair. It was also horrible, as the wine did not numb anything. In fact, it was harder to bear it at all. With every movement, I became dizzier. When he was done and removed himself, the queasiness became too much to control, and I vomited all over his feet. He yelled and cursed, moved away while I hobbled towards the nearest sofa, sitting down and curling into a ball, letting myself recover. Zeus charged from the room, swearing.

The next day, I learned that hangovers are much worse when coupled with childbirth. So it was that Eris was born to the world, my final daughter, the goddess of strife. As she grew older, she seemed to favour emotional and psychological manipulation above other diversions, a suitable trait for the goddess of enmity. She took great pleasure in it. The only ones who could withstand her tricks of the mind were Zeus and me, whom she respected or feared too much, and Athene, who was too intelligent and wise to fall bait to Eris and even beat her at it, which Eris hated. I scolded my daughter for her behaviour, but ultimately it was what made her happy. It was who she was, and I could not change that, try as I might, just like I could not change her father.

Following my drunken episode, Zeus announced to the court: "I have been aggrieved to hear of the debauchery that has been taking place at these Dionysian so-called parties on Olympos. Therefore, it is only fitting to introduce measures to prevent these disgusting crimes. These attacks cannot go on."

Everyone was transfixed, looking at him, waiting.

"Goddesses and nymphs, women on Earth below, must be on their guard to protect their virtue. They must learn to take responsibility for their lack of judgement. While they are not inclined to reason, they must try to retain the little they have. And so, from now on, I decree that any mortal female caught drinking wine will be put to death. Any goddess will be exiled," Zeus declared.

I didn't look at him. I was not shocked.

Murmurings rumbled through the court.

In Heaven, wine and the parties of Dionysos belonged to gods. On Earth, only courtesans were permitted to attend parties and drink wine, as they were not considered to have any repute worth saving while still providing a necessary service. Meanwhile, citizen women were allowed to worship Dionysos at parties but were still prohibited wine. Non-religious drinking parties became known as symposia and were exclusively all-male. As of that night, mead became the female drink. So it was that I could never get lost again or run away in my mind from my husband.

17: THYONE

I hovered at Dionysos's door once again. I had not seen him in several days. There was also no occasion when I could have taken him aside to tell him of Ariadne's plight. For some reason, I felt nervous. Part of me believed that bringing Ariadne and Dionysos together and making them reconcile would have been the better course. Still, I had tried that with Aphrodite and Hephaistos in the past, and it had failed me miserably. I knew that the only way to make happiness was to allow it to happen in whatever was enjoyed. Ariadne and Dionysos did not enjoy each other's company. They were very different creatures. That had been the long and short of it. They had barely been wed a month. Maybe they would have fallen into a stride of some kind, but there was no certainty of it.

The trouble was that I did not know Dionysos well. We were acquaintances, closer to being hostile work colleagues than relatives. I hoped he would bring the matter up himself, and I could take it from there. However, it also occurred to me that he might not care enough to ask about her.

Stop dawdling! I scolded myself. *No queen lingers at the door like this.*

I knocked on the door. "Dionysos? Dionysos, are you inside?"

No answer, so I tried again, knocking a bit harder. "Dionysos?"

With the knocking, the door creaked as it opened slightly. I pushed it a little further, calling out his name as I did so. Again, no response.

Breathing deeply, I committed to quietly trespassing. The walls were covered in ivy and burnt-out torches. The air stank of wine. I passed the archway which led into his bedchamber and jumped back in horror.

There he was, sprawled on the bedclothes, covered in spilt wine, a golden goblet fallen onto the floor from his open palm. His eyes were half-open — I could see the whites — and he was dribbling saliva from his mouth.

"Dionysos?" I cried out, running towards him.

"What? Woah!" he snorted, lifting his head.

I sat back, breathing a sigh of relief. "Oh, you are awake."

"Well, I am now," he grumbled, rubbing his eyes.

"I am sorry. I saw you lying there. I thought you were possibly dead."

He raised an eyebrow at me. "I am a god."

"Demigod," I reminded him. "At any rate, I thought you were unconscious."

"What are you doing here?" he asked, struggling to sit up.

I licked my lips. "I have come because I must talk to you about something."

His eyes began roaming around his bed in a slight frown. He checked under the pillows and sheets soaked with red wine. Then he glanced down the side of the bed and saw what he needed. Reaching down, he picked up his fallen goblet.

"Go on," he said, stretching for an amphora on the bedside table and filling his goblet.

I frowned. "Should you really be drinking so much?"

He huffed, speech slightly slurred. "Should you really be here at all?"

I blushed. "You should know Ariadne has sought my advice."

No emotion overcame his face at the mention of her. He took a sip of wine.

"She is unhappy. She says she receives no love or care from you, who fussed over choosing her. She says her bond with you is one of servitude rather than marriage. I am here to ask you to improve your treatment of her, so your marriage can be a success."

He pointed his index finger at me from the hand holding the goblet. "You know how to mind your own business, do you not?"

"I am concerned about my family."

He narrowed his eyes. "I am not your family, though. Am I?"

I was a little hurt by that. I did not know what to say to him.

"That was rude of me," he muttered, glancing away. "You are my family. You are my father's sister and wife and my mother's great-grandmother."

I tilted my head. "I also looked after you as an infant. I cared for you. I put clothes on you. I washed you, made sure you were comfortable and had all that you needed."

He slowly put his goblet down, focusing intently as he looked at me. "You also burnt my mother alive."

"Semele asked Zeus to reveal his true form. He agreed," I shot back, offended.

He scowled. "Without your help, my mother would have never asked him."

I rose from the bed, realising this was a waste of my strength. "I am sorry for what happened to your mother, but I did not make her do anything. Neither did I force you to select Ariadne for your bride. If you are looking to place blame, I suggest you look higher than me. None of this would have happened without Zeus. I did not come here for an argument but to inform you of your wife's unhappiness —"

He shook his head. "Stop, please."

I faltered and let him speak.

He sighed. "I have been a boar where Ariadne is concerned. I will try to do better with her. However, it is difficult."

"What do you mean?"

He shrugged. "I do not expect you to understand."

"Try," I encouraged him.

He hesitated before speaking: "I wake up daily with hate for myself and for my life. And so, it is difficult to treat others well."

I felt a twinge of regret in my chest. "If I could bring your mother back, I would."

"What do you think I have been trying to do all these years?" he chuckled drily. "All the countries and kingdoms, all to find a way to get to her, but I failed."

"I thought you travelled to prove yourself to the mortals."

He scoffed. "Please. That merely happened along the way, but it was never my goal."

I sat down beside him again. "Is that what you are trying to overcome — the failure of your efforts?"

He shook his head, sighing. "No. It is not just that."

"Then what?"

He smiled sadly. "You would not like me if I told you."

"You should have more faith in me."

He hesitated and then spoke. "On my adventures, in the land of Phrygia, I came to a stream. It was a beautiful place, surrounded by trees. The banks were lined with roses, something I had never seen before. The water was a gorgeous aquamarine colour. I could not help but get in and swim."

I smiled at the thought.

"Afterwards, I hunted in the moonlight and in the woods, I came across a youth, just younger than me, with golden curls, rosy cheeks, and bright eyes. His voice was still sweet and melodic. His skin glistened under the stars. He was perfect.

"I did not want to scare him away, so I took the form of a human man and befriended him. I asked him who his father was or if he was another god in disguise. But he never answered or enlightened me. I found out his name: Ampelos, but no more than that. He only ever sang for me and played music, and never were there sounds more beautiful to my ears. Then I could not listen to anything else. Sometimes we wrestled together. I met with him frequently but found my spirits much lower when I was not with him. I do not know if I was in love with him. I know that I was lonely when I was not in his presence. I know that I missed him. Whenever I saw him with other men, I felt jealousy of the most tremendous force. I know my worst fear was that he would die. I even feared that he might be taken from me somehow, that I would lose him.

"One day, we went hunting, and my worst fear was realised. After we had been separated, I found him lying dead in the ground, killed by a bull. So, I dressed him properly, putting buskins on his feet. I sprinkled roses and lilies over his corpse and placed a garland on his head. I put a thyrsos in one of his hands and then gave him my purple robe before cutting off a lock of my hair and placing it on him. I had ambrosia which I poured into his wounds. Even dead, he was still beautiful to me. There was even a slight smile on his face.

"I was joined by Eros, who comforted me and turned my beloved Ampelos into a grapevine by the river. I tried to hold it, to bring him back to the form of a boy, dead or not. However, the grapes just burst, and it was from that I got my famous wine."

I stared at him in shock. I hardly knew what to say. "Dionysos, I am so sorry."

His tears dropped into the goblet. "Now, the only way to get close to him is to drink."

I leaned forward and took the goblet from his hand. "But it will not bring him back from the Underworld. Savour the gift he has given you in his afterlife. Protect it. Share with others, including Ariadne, this love you felt. You have already started that journey. Do not stop now. In the meantime, cherish your memories with him and make new ones with those around you."

"It is easier said than done, but I will try my best."

I searched for something more helpful to say. "You could try to descend to the Underworld, to retrieve him, or even your mother. You would need to consult with Hermes since he is the only god to regularly pass through that realm."

Dionysos frowned at me. "You think I should keep trying?"

"If it is what will make you happy. We must never stop trying to be happy, must we?"

He hesitated, and then pointed out: "If I succeed, I shall bring Semele here to court."

I placed my hand on his and squeezed it tightly. "I would expect nothing less, and I would do my utmost to make her feel welcome. However, first, you must get her back. No one has ever returned a dead mortal soul from the Underworld, not even a god."

"I know that. I will try all the same."

And so, I left with a better understanding of Dionysos, hopeful he would take my advice.

After speaking to Ariadne, Dionysos departed the following month for the Underworld after receiving advice from Hermes on how to retrieve his mother. There are many versions of how he did this, as whenever he was asked about it, his drunken mind would tell a different story each time. A little embellishment here, a detour there. Then others added their own elaborations. Some even claimed it happened while he was still travelling before coming to Olympos. Others said a mortal shepherd called Prosymnos helped Dionysos cross to the Underworld if he could become Dionysos's lover in exchange. However, Prosymnos died before this could ever happen, much to the anguish of Dionysos. Some claim he went to Haides after the time of Herakles, that Herakles had bound Kerberos, the three-headed hound of Haides, in advance of Dionysos's arrival and that Dionysos escaped with his mother up from the deepest waters of the Great Sea. However, Herakles was not yet born, whatever the means of their departure. And so, no one knows how he brought his mother back from the Kingdom of the Dead.

In my opinion, the most likely way he retrieved Semele was through diplomacy: once he arrived in the Underworld, he was escorted into Haides's palace, much like we were, and there he petitioned Haides to return his mother to him. Haides may even have been pleased to meddle by sending Semele back to Zeus and me.

Before Semele arrived on Olympos, Dionysos gave her his purple cloak so she would not be scorned for appearing so underdressed. She was still as young as she had been when I had seen her last. However, she was nowhere near as arrogant or silly as the girl I had met. Now called Thyone — a new name for a new life — she was just as beautiful as ever and looked exactly as she had on the day she had died, with her long dark hair flowing down her back, braids running through her locks, and dressed for bed.

I was nervous, expecting no courtesy from her. Still, it seemed the Princess of Thebes had grown wiser from her death, which made her worthy of a place in the Olympian court.

When Thyone walked into the courtroom on her son's arm, one could tell that her soul had aged from its time in the Underworld. She smiled at everyone with kindness and curtseyed low in great respect for Zeus and me. "Lord Zeus, my king. Lady Hera, my queen."

"Thyone, once Semele of Thebes, you are as beautiful as ever," Zeus commented imperiously. "You are welcome here; free to stay for as long as possible. Your son has been yearning for your company, and his wife, Ariadne, could use your guiding hand."

Thyone smiled. "It is a great honour to join your court, Lord Zeus."

And so, she moved in with Dionysos and helped Ariadne in her duties as a wife.

In a matter of days, Dionysos reduced the number of parties he hosted to once a week. They started producing wine as a large-scale industry rather than just for domestic consumption in his rooms. He also began giving advice for those wishing to imbibe wine. He even created a trained chorus, open to all Olympos citizens who could perform lyric poetry, dance, and sing at Zeus's balls and feasts. Then he began to promote his cult on Earth, centred around the Great Dionysia, an annual festival where theatrical competitions were held. He composed several plays himself, which he commissioned to be performed in the Olympian palace. Once his actors and band members began to get paid, there was a charge for seats at his plays. Yet many were happy to pay. In time, Dionysos's theatre was built on Olympos, a regularly frequented place during the calendar.

He was finally at peace of some kind. He started looking for joy in the world rather than just being able to see darkness and loneliness. The wine was still his favourite drink, as Ampelos had been his great love, but no longer did Dionysos turn to it to numb pain, as he was able to turn to Thyone for any care and kindness he needed. He even developed a sense of purpose and wanted to sit on the council of the gods, except all twelve thrones were taken. With all other court positions too lowly for a son of Zeus, it seemed the god of wine was about to fall into another pit of despair when I received a visit from a long-forgotten foe.

"You were right," a female voice said.

I was writing at my desk. I looked to see Hestia standing in the doorway of my bedchamber. I had an immediate sense of dread. "What are you doing here, and what are you talking about?"

She stepped into my bedchamber, her chin held high. "I have come to try to make peace once again. Last time you claimed you still felt the effects of my betrayal, as you put it. I hope now you will realise that I do not deserve your censure any longer," she said. Her voice was soft but firm.

"What do you think you deserve?" I said, putting my pen down.

"Forgiveness," she replied simply after a moment of hesitation. "I did wrong by you. I sided with Zeus, who has hurt not just you but everyone I care about. I was blind at the time. I did not want strife, but it only created more."

I looked at her warily.

"I truly am sorry," she continued, looking at me. "It has taken some time, perhaps too long, to apologise. I want to be your sister again, someone you can rely upon to help. I want to feel like my family accepts me again. Perhaps you have not seen it nor cared to, but my brothers and sisters, nieces and nephews shun me. I am alone nearly all of the time. I have no friends and no family."

Her demeanour was downcast. She looked broken.

I pursed my lips as I considered her request. I could not help but pity her. After my turbulent time with Demeter, I was tired of being at odds with my sisters. "I know what that feels like, and it is awful. I do not want to be cruel anymore. So, I will forgive you," I said, letting out a heavy breath. "If you truly regret the choice you made."

She stared at me, eyes shining in disbelief. "I do," she croaked.

"Well then, let us consider the matter settled and buried firmly in the past," I said, giving her a small smile and standing up from the desk.

Hestia rushed forward and flung her arms around me. We embraced once more as sisters. Then she stood back, wiping a tear from her cheek. "The truth is that although I am one of the Kronides, the eldest of us, I have never felt like I should be. Most days, I feel like an imposter in court. I am not of strong character like the rest of you. I am so indecisive — I can never choose a side. I am too…" She trailed off.

"In the middle," I finished quietly.

She nodded, blushing.

"I understand that."

"So I have come to a decision."

"A decision? Hestia, are you feeling all right?"

She giggled. "Yes, and on this one matter, I am certain of where I stand." Her smile dropped. "I am going to give up my throne."

"What?" My mouth opened in shock. I never thought I would ever hear those words from a fellow Olympian.

"I shall give it to Dionysos."

My eyes widened. "What?" I repeated, more disbelieving this time.

She shrugged. "Well, why not? He wants a place as one of the twelve Olympians, and I do not. He has much more to offer Hellenic society than I do. It seems like the perfect solution to two problems."

There was a sinking feeling in my stomach. "Hestia, you would lose all say in how the world is governed."

"Have I ever used that privilege? I cannot remember when I suggested or argued a point. There is no need for me personally to have that seat. As a child of Kronos, I will always be an integral part of this government, an advisor and peacekeeper when needed. But I have always been an observer rather than a doer. I have no love for politics or debate. I am much happier without such conflicts. I need peace to be happy, not the perennial problems of a government minister. Without such responsibility, I can turn my mind to matters I truly care about."

I now looked at her with newfound admiration and realisation that I was a fraud. I had always thought I had carried on the character of Rhea, Queen of the Titans. Yet, as I looked at my eldest sister, I realised it was Hestia who held that same countenance of serenity and tranquillity. It seemed she was the only one of the Kronides to have her mother's disposition. It was almost as if she had transformed into my mother before my eyes.

"If this is what your heart truly desires, I will fully support you in this decision." I fought down a wave of emotion.

"Thank you," she said softly.

The next day, Hestia stepped down from her throne and gave it to Dionysos.

18: ALKMENE

When it happened, I was sitting in my bedchamber, getting ready for the day, with my nymphs doing my hair and applying colour to my face. I thought I had imagined it, that I was going mad, but then I heard it again — someone calling my name repeatedly.

Hera? Hera! Hera.

I scanned my surroundings for whoever it was. "What was that?" I asked.

"My lady?" a nymph replied, sounding confused.

"Someone said my name," I said, irritated that she had not been paying attention.

The other nymph responded after a hesitation. "We heard nothing, my lady."

I frowned. "Leave me."

They dropped their tools and curtseyed before scurrying from the room.

Hera, someone whispered in my ears. *Hera?*

I got up from my chair. The sound was unmistakable to me. However, I was entirely alone in my bedchamber. Nevertheless, the voice kept calling. I even left my room to search for it but in vain. I heard it again that afternoon. Yet whenever I got up to look, there was no one there.

It became a huge distraction and kept me from performing most of my duties. I missed audiences with courtiers and was often absent from the palace for days. I was convinced and told them the truth: I kept hearing someone calling my name.

My family became concerned. Zeus would often tell me to go and lie down, even if I did something as small as putting my head in my hands or rubbing my forehead when I had a headache. He would sometimes rebuke me and tell me not to bother everyone with my maladies. Sometimes I found myself lying at dinner or in meetings, claiming I had heard the voice, so I could be excused. It was no surprise they all grew tired of my complaining and that Zeus dismissed me entirely from the courtroom. I did not protest this decision too much, although I thought it was unfair. On the upside, I did not have to stay with Zeus for too long at any one time.

One evening, growing weary of the company, I was about to claim such a falsehood to try and leave early when Zeus rose to his feet.

The whole dining hall fell silent.

I huffed, knowing I would not be able to leave the room until he had finished addressing the courtiers present.

"My noble Olympians and esteemed courtiers," he began with a smile. "It gives me great pleasure to deliver news to you of my forthcoming son this evening."

A new bastard. My heart sank.

The room filled with excited cheers and clapping at the news.

"He shall be a demigod renowned for his deeds and named after them, too," my husband went on, grinning from ear to ear.

I looked down, face hot, trying to appear unperturbed by the news. As accustomed as I was to these declarations, I did not think I would ever become used to the humiliation. I caught the pitying glances of some of my family members while those courtiers unfamiliar with the circumstances of my marriage looked at me warily, probably wondering which poor woman and her child I would hunt down and torture now.

He waved his hand in showmanship. "This day, he shall be born from Alkmene, a mortal woman of Thebes and priestess of my wife and queen, Hera. He will be one of a set of twins, the other the product of her husband, Amphitryon, in whose form I came to his wife several months ago and lay with her for three days until the real Amphitryon returned!"

While many minor gods and courtiers whooped and laughed around the room, enjoying the theatre of it, I felt a rising sense of revulsion. I spared a glance at Demeter beside me. She had closed her eyes, also trying to hide her disgust. Only a few goddesses and nymphs wore smiles, nervous ones.

Zeus made a shushing gesture with his hands. "Now, what makes this child so different from the rest, you ask? I have been told of a prophecy which predicts that my new son will be of such immense strength that he will rule all those around him by nature. He will be stronger, faster, and of a far more agile mind than any hero, a worthy brother to even the best of the Olympian gods. Is such a child not to be eagerly awaited? A demigod worthy of his heritage!"

The room filled with cheers and applause. The roaring response from the courtiers grew into a deafening stamping of feet and banging on tables, a loud noise worthy of the promised superstar. The court of Olympos raised a toast.

After the announcement, I sat on my bed, feeling bereft. How had I not sensed Zeus's infidelity when he was with Alkmene? Even without his declarations, my instincts as the goddess of marriage often let me know which beds he had occupied. Yet I had not seen this one coming at all.

And so, I sought Zeus out for a private audience, asking the guard outside his office door whether or not he was available to see me. Receiving a curt nod of acknowledgement, I opened the door. I was determined to stay composed, hard as it would be.

"Hera, what is the matter this time?" Zeus asked wearily upon seeing me. He looked up from his desk where, under the light of a candle, he had been scribbling a decree upon a scroll.

I took a deep breath before speaking. "My lord, forgive me for speaking so bluntly, but this latest announcement of yours troubles me. You now have another child to crown besides those I have given you and raised for you, and you have declared him to be the greatest of them — a half-ling? What am I supposed to think and feel after such words? What is so special about this one?" I had to bite my tongue not to say 'bastard'.

Zeus huffed, dropped his quill, and sat back in his chair. "You always need an explanation, do you not? Very well. The next demigod of my line shall rule over Argos and will start a bloodline which shall spread throughout the lands and through the ages until my direct descendants rule over all Hellas. That is the point," he clarified.

"However, this will not bar the way for any of my divine children who dwell on Olympos. Not only that but there is also a prophecy of a war on the horizon. There are monsters abroad who would see the Olympians destroyed. We may need all the help we can get. This child will help us."

I swallowed, my throat dry. "Is that a certainty?"

He raised his eyebrows at me, throwing up his hands. "Yes, Hera. Which part do you not understand? I would swear on it, but it is bound to happen anyway, so I see little point. Does this make matters clearer for you, wife? The coming of my next child is no hindrance to the rest of my children in their entitlements."

Already a plan was forming in my head. "Yes, my lord."

He waved me away. "Good. Now, be gone. I have many issues to attend to."

Curtseying, I left the room, steadfast that Zeus would not have his way. To call this bastard greater than all his children, even Ares, before the entire court? That I could not abide.

Immediately, I set off, going through the air to Thebes. I took my daughter Eileithyia, goddess of childbirth, with me to the house of Amphitryon, Alkmene's husband. While the poor woman was going into labour, I instructed Eileithyia to sit at the end of her birthing bed with her legs crossed to prevent Alkmene from giving birth. Meanwhile, I rushed west to Tiryns, a stronghold founded by the greatest earthly hero Perseus, another son of Zeus. I admit I had no great loyalty to the Tirynian dynasty. Still, I knew there was to be a grandson of Perseus, a descendant of my husband, who would become King of Argos.

In my spite and determination to have my revenge for yet another public humiliation, I delivered the boy, Eurystheus, myself to make sure he survived his entrance into the world. He would become King of Tiryns and the surrounding lands. I was delighted at how pale Zeus's face was when he heard the news delivered by messenger to the court. He glared thunderously at me out of the corner of his eye, but he was not about to turn on his word, so he declared Eurystheus King of Argos.

Much to my irritation, soon after Eurystheus's birth, Galanthis, the maidservant of Alkmene, saw Eileithyia and told her that the lady of the house had already given birth. How this maid had seen my daughter, I know not; perhaps she had some supernatural power, or Zeus had inspired her to trick the goddess of childbirth. At any rate, upon hearing Galanthis's lies, Eileithyia jumped back in surprise, uncrossing her legs. Then the exhausted Alkmene let out a cry of pain, and

Herakles was born into the world. Unsurprisingly, I transformed Galanthis into a weasel for her interference.

No more than a couple of days later, Athene came to me, knocking on my door. I welcomed them in and found, to my surprise, a wailing baby swaddled in white linen in their arms. It was a fat little thing with a bulbous head.

"I did not know what to do," Athene said, distress evident in their voice. "I found it lying on the mountainside and —" they broke off, their voice catching. "Who would do such a thing?"

Pity overcoming my shock, I gently took the baby from them. Turning away, I brought the baby inside, rocking it gently. "Many mothers leave their daughters to perish," I said.

"Why girls?" Athene followed me inside, closing the door.

"They are not as important as boys, not as strong and left ignorant through lack of education. They will one day leave the family home to become part of another's household and, until that day, for fathers, they are simply an extra mouth to feed, a financial drain, and a source of shame upon the household that his wife cannot produce an heir. Exposing them to the elements and wolves is much cheaper and more efficient."

Looking down at the baby, the silver eyes and short wisps of golden curls upon its head seemed slightly familiar. Curious, I lifted the linen from its legs and peered inside. "This one is a boy," I gasped.

"Really?" Athene came forward, surprise evident in their voice. "What father would expose their own son?"

I shook my head. "I do not know."

The little boy lifted his legs and wailed even louder.

"Well, he is fine and strong. What does he want?" They asked worriedly.

"Milk, most likely," I guessed, unravelling the baby from the rest of its swaddling clothes and handing him to Athene.

They took him hesitantly. "Are you going to…"

"Yes," I said. "I cannot stand crying babies for many reasons. Pity. Noise." I took my breast from my peplos and lifted the baby's mouth to it. Contentedly silenced, he began to suck, swallowing happily and eagerly.

Meanwhile, Athene turned away, blushing to see such a sight. I laughed at their reaction. "It is a perfectly natural thing."

Athene shuffled uncomfortably, still not looking my way. "I know."

"He must have been starving," I whispered, shaking my head. I smiled at him. Then a sharp pain shot through my chest. "Ouch!" I cried, looking at the baby who had latched too firmly onto my nipple, squeezing down hard. "Get him off!"

Turning to me, unsure of where to look, Athene carefully removed the baby from my chest and hugged him to themself.

I saw both ichor and milk dribble from my breast. Hissing in pain, I tried to dab away the ichor with my hands. "You must take the child back," I snapped.

Athene stared at me, horrified. "It would kill him."

I shook my head. "You misunderstand me. Take him back to his mother."

"Hera, I do not know who the mother is."

"Figure it out. You are the clever one here," I huffed, still in discomfort.

"Very well." They cradled the baby in their arms. "At least he has stopped crying."

"Go quickly," I instructed. "His mother will be missing him."

Athene nodded and hurried from the room.

Frowning down at my bleeding bosom, I wiped the still-leaking blood and milk. Disgusted, I cast the liquids from my palm into the air. Little did I know that the milk would seep out on the waves of the winds into the atmosphere and create the Milky Way among the stars and that the baby had been no random infant Athene had found by chance.

It took me hours to figure it out, and it was only when I went to the courtroom to attend the government that I approached my husband and saw those same grey eyes. That was when I knew, with my ichor turning cold, that I had just given milk to my husband's latest bastard.

I confronted Athene about it, but they denied knowing the baby's true identity. I was unsure whether to believe them. Athene was Wisdom, after all; wily enough when they wanted to be. When I pressed the matter, they told me of a woman they had seen wandering the woods outside Thebes, weeping and moaning about the loss of her little Herakles.

"Herakles?" I repeated, bewildered.

Athene nodded. "Yes. Originally Alkaios, the child was renamed Herakles, 'the glory of Hera'. She explained it was a peace offering to you, a pleading to show the child mercy and her. She said her husband wanted the infant dead, so your wrath would not fall on them."

I balled my fists, furious at how the hellion had been delivered to my arms and nursed at my breast, my kindness exploited.

"What shall you do?"

"Never you mind," I growled.

I bit my lower lip and shook my head as I paced around my bedchamber later that day, glancing out the window to the world of Hellas beyond. About the child, I had no doubt, but Alkmene? Was she involved in my revenge?

"No," I whispered to myself.

Alkmene, one of my own priestesses, had been raped. Zeus had admitted it himself. So, she would be spared.

It was early morning as I peered into the cot, tilting my head as I inspected the bastard within, which I had suckled a few months previously. He was lying motionless with his eyes closed and his fists held tightly to his chest. He grew quickly compared to his twin brother in the cot beside him, both now eight months old. He had some blonde curls, Zeus's trademark from his filthy seed. He was clearly his father's son.

I had pondered how horrible it would be for Zeus's pride and joy to suddenly be taken at such a young age and how tragically raw the pain would be for Zeus if this child were to perish so soon. I imagined all sorts of ways I might snuff out his little life. I knew I had already spent too much time prevaricating. It was not that I lacked resolve. No, I had to wait for Zeus to be suitably distracted so that he would not be suspicious.

Stepping back from the cradle, I looked from Herakles to his brother. I would not let a mere mortal thwart me. I cast my hands over Herakles, conjuring up two long black serpents. I tossed them quickly into the cot. Heart beating fast, I eagerly waited and watched, expecting to see them devour the child within moments, wrapping around his neck or whole little body and squeezing him until his soft flesh burst, spilling those mortal blood and guts, a genuine horror to await his mother.

However, his twin, in his terror, screamed out and alerted his brother to the danger. With a deftness of speed I had never witnessed, his tiny hands grabbed the necks of the snakes and squeezed tightly. Letting out an amused gurgle, he smashed their heads together repeatedly until the snakes became limp and unmoving. Their eyes lost their evil sparkle. His little white fingers released their grip, and the reptiles collapsed beside him, lifeless. He gurgled happily and clapped his hands, kicking his feet and grabbing at the air in front of me as if he wanted to be lifted up.

Horrified, I looked into the boy's silver eyes, staring back up at me with curious innocence. I realised it would take more than a couple of reptiles to destroy this new abomination, this wretch.

I returned to Olympos, more annoyed than usual. How could I have possibly lost against a baby? I paced my bedchamber. I could not fathom it. Was he as invincible as Zeus had claimed? However, he was not immortal. That much was certain. There had to be a way.

19: ECHO

That night I could not sleep, the matter of my husband's latest child taking up all the space in my mind. I found it impossible to relax.

Hera? Hera. Hera! That awful little voice called to me, among everything else.

I cursed it for being so distracting. However, in doing that, a thought came to me. This voice had indeed been a distraction, I realised. It had become worse lately, genuinely maddening, disrupting my sleep. Sometimes, I found myself waiting for it; whether it was there or not, the voice began to occupy my every moment. There was no peace to be had from it. It had led me away from recognising my husband's infidelity before his announcement.

Hera. Hera? Hera!

I frowned and turned my head towards the window, for, this time, it was definitely coming from outside.

Without a second thought, I jumped from my bed, giving chase on foot. I bolted through the trees, running faster than ever. The breeze blasted through my hair. Under cover of night, I leapt over logs and past bushes, sensing the barriers in the air before I was met with them.

The song in my head, calling my name, was reduced to giggles and panting breath, running away from me.

Yet I was faster. Feeling myself drawing near, I reached out my hand and snatched whatever was in front of me. I grabbed a fistful of hair.

I skidded to a halt, yanking the creature back as well.

The voice yelped. Whoever it was cried out.

Dragging the hair, I pulled it to a clearing upon which the moon was shining. I shoved it out onto the grass and saw exactly who the voice belonged to.

A mountain nymph, an Oread. It was evident from the leaves tangled in her wild hair, the flesh of her limbs covered in a layer of mud and patches of tree bark and moss leaves growing out of her fingernails and a dress made of ivy. She had markings on her face, large freckles around her hairline and on the contours of her face, and large brown spots on her eyelids. Her eyes glinted under the moonlight, dark brown like the forest trees.

"Give me your name," I ordered, enraged.

"I have no name," came her reply, her voice floating in the wind around me still. It was soft and melodic. "Only talent." She smirked with thin lips.

"Is it a talent to invade a person's mind and drive them insane?" I demanded.

She gave me a cheeky grin and raised an eyebrow. "I am good at it."

I felt my temper rising. "I do not care about that. Why come after me?"

She pursed her lips together, humming. "Do I need a reason, my lady?"

"Unless you want to make this worse for yourself, yes," I snapped. *The cheek!* "To torment your queen is quite an audacious act."

I approached her and grabbed her jaw. "An attack even. You have heard the tales of my victims. Almost everyone has. Many would not dare come after me."

I narrowed my eyes at her. "Unless they have something greater to fear," I whispered.

For a moment, I wondered if I was speaking nonsense. However, the sudden and very small widening of her eyes, the slight recoil of her back and the tensing up of her shoulders assured me that I was correct. She was taking orders from someone greater than me. I knew that the only possible option was my own husband.

I was pleased to see the absolute terror in her eyes. "I already know everything I need," I told her. "My darling husband must have ordered you to distract me whenever he went off with his mistresses. Am I correct?"

She gulped and nodded slightly. "Do not kill me. I beg you, my lady."

That felon.

"I am not going to kill you. You were following orders," I hissed.

She nodded and whimpered, her body slumping in relief save for her head which I was still holding firmly. She closed her eyes, and tears rolled down her cheeks.

"Yet you enjoyed it. You have enjoyed contributing to the breakdown of my marriage." I quickly moved my hand to her neck, seizing hold of it. She squawked in distress, but I cut her off, my fingers squeezing her tiny throat.

"For that, your pretty little voice will never again speak of its own volition. It will be trapped and condemned to forever repeat the utterings of others. For this, I give you a name; that is all you will ever know." I leaned in and whispered in her ear. "Echo."

Then I let go, whirling around and leaving her standing there, choking, coughing and spluttering, clutching her throat and staring at me in terror as my curse came to life.

At first, the matter of Echo infuriated me, for if Zeus had put in place a strategy to distract me from his disloyal antics with Alkmene, there were bound to be other mistresses and bastards. As I have said before, Zeus was nothing if not thorough. Then I was ecstatic, proud of myself. My past punishments of his mistresses had come to something after all. Either he had realised the tediousness and tiresomeness of having me hunt them down, or he felt it was no longer worth risking his children's lives. Either way, I had achieved something. Then again, maybe this was more problematic — it would now take more effort to discover the new ways in which he was betraying me. But at least he was scared. He had to be. It was the only thing that made sense. He was afraid of me. How astonishing was that? Suddenly the birth of Herakles was not so difficult to bear after all.

However, this newfound knowledge was not enough to stop me from turning my hand against that bastard child again. He could not live as Zeus's favourite son, not when he had five others to pick from, including those I had given him. Herakles was a grown man, a fully-fledged demigod, living in Thebes with his wife and children when I decided to visit him next.

Landing on the cobblestones of Thebes, surrounded by the cold night and under the watchful eyes of the stars above, I approached his house, a large, white building surrounded by gates, torches mounted by the door, with a fierce hound guarding the entrance. I bypassed the guard dog easily, donning a cover of invisibility, dulling the beast's senses, and letting it fall to the ground in a heavy sleep. Then, levitating into the air to peer in through a small high window on the outer wall, I spied into the dining room of the great Herakles. There I saw him eating with his wife and children.

He had grown into an enormous man, much like his father. With incredible height, he bulged with muscle. He had a fluffy beard of blonde hair. There were no lines around his grey eyes. This was a person of power, I recognised. A true heir of Zeus.

Sitting with him around the table, laden with platters of food, were two boys and two girls, his sons and daughters, all likely under the age of ten. Each child was supple and bursting with energy. One of his boys had not yet left his swaddling clothes and enthusiastically smashed his food into mush on the table. In contrast, the older ones smiled and laughed with each other at ridiculous mundane jokes and tales.

His wife, a pretty little thing, small and slender, sat across from Herakles. This was Megara, the daughter of Kreon, the King of Thebes. It was a wonder how lying with such a husband every night and bearing four of his children had not broken her tiny frame in half. She had dark brown hair, done up neatly. Her clothes and jewellery told me of her status.

"Herakles," I heard Megara say, addressing her husband. "Do tell us how you crossed paths with the embodiments of Vice and Virtue."

The children joined in, eagerly begging for the tale to be told again.

I rolled my eyes.

So the famed son of Zeus began retelling, in a deep voice that seemed to resonate from every part of his massive physique, of his meeting when he was a young man with the two goddesses of sin and goodness, how he was made to choose between a life of difficulty and one of ease; and how he naturally, being a pious demigod, chose the former as opposed to the latter.

I nearly vomited at the self-righteousness. I refused to believe that any man could be that virtuous, especially the son of the King of Olympos.

When he finished his tale, his children gasped with awe at their father. Megara batted her lashes at him, reaching across the table and squeezing her husband's hand, joining in the chorus of praise at his actions, saying she could not have been luckier in marriage.

At the sight, a fire of fury ignited within me, my soul like a coiled spring, tight with tension. I pushed myself away from the window.

Am I proud of what happened next? No. Yet, at the time, to me, it was the right thing.

I waited until Megara had gone upstairs to her quarters, her children following close behind and until the man of the house retired to his bedchamber downstairs to guard his sleeping family, blowing out all the torches on his way. Then, once I thought they were asleep, I quietly unlatched the front door, stepping over the sleeping dog, who snored so terribly I almost feared that sound alone would wake the family. However, when there was no noise to be heard other than the creature in its slumber, I tiptoed down the hall towards Herakles's room. I opened the door and stepped inside using my magic, invisible in the darkness. I entered and stood over his bed.

The enormous man rumbled with snoring in his sleep, much like his dog, but louder. I could see the disgusting resemblance between him and my husband. Trembling slightly with the excitement of rage and anticipation, I leaned down. My mouth hovered above his ear, the curse on my tongue. I spoke it softly and let it corrupt his senses in his sleep.

Suddenly, the snoring turned into a roar. Herakles shot from his bed in a fierce bolt, nearly knocking me over, with a flash of lightning in his eyes, red anger all over his face.

I scrambled out of the way, falling to the floor.

Herakles stormed out of his room, grabbing an extinguished torch from its place on the wall. He raced up the stepladder towards his family.

Getting to my feet, I rushed out of the house. I slammed the front door behind me and ran out onto the streets.

The air filled with the terrified screams of his wife and children, reverberating out of the high windows as their beloved husband and father bludgeoned them to death, smashing their skulls and destroying the beauty he had created.

I could imagine the splatter of their brains on the walls and their blood dripping through the floorboards.

20: HERAKLES

Poor Herakles. He had committed one of the most heinous acts in existence. Killing any family member was known as a blood crime. The murderer was so thoroughly stained he could only receive pardon on Earth through rigorous punishments, often by enslavement. With immense satisfaction, I watched as he wept and wailed his way, with a broken heart and spirit, to the Oracle of Delphi to atone for his sin through prayer to Apollo, who, horrified at Herakles's crime, no matter the reason why, sent him to King Eurystheus of Argos for redemption.

King Eurystheus had grown up jealous of his relative's prowess and bravery, jealous of the love and favour showed by Zeus, and jealous of the renown Zeus had bragged of and promised. He could not believe his good fortune that Herakles had so monumentally destroyed his own destiny. Eurystheus was more than happy to put manners on his cousin. Indeed, it was easy for me to inspire the King of Argos to work my will against Herakles.

I watched as Herakles presented himself to Eurystheus; the king placed high on his throne above the shamed Herakles prostrate on the floor before him. Copreus, the king's herald, announced ten trials, which would be his punishment. Far and wide, he would have to labour but only then, and only if he succeeded in completing all ten, would he be purified of his sin. I decided to stay on Earth to watch his demise.

First, there was the Nemean lion, a beast of such might and savagery even its name filled humans with terror. None had ever survived it. Eurystheus ordered Herakles not to return unless he had the fleece of the lion with him.

I watched as the demigod attacked the beast with arrows. To his frustration, they bounced off it, for its golden hide could not be pierced by any mortal weapon. However, it seemed that Herakles had inherited his father's mind for strategy. He cornered the lion in a cave of two entrances, beating the poor creature with his club of the olive tree before twisting its neck with his hands. Then he skinned the lion's corpse with its own claws, taking its skin for protection and as a sign of his strength.

How the fur shone in the moonlight reminded me of the lions I had raised on Samos. So, after Herakles had departed the cave, I approached the dead beast, feeling sorrow mounting in my heart. I saw the bumps on his back, mounds of bone protruding from its spine, which had never grown into wings like its mother, the gryphon of Samos. Realising it was a cub I had cared for myself, I could not help but burst into tears and kneel beside it in mourning before taking it upon myself to bury it.

Filled with fresh anger for the impudent mortal, I had Eurystheus send Herakles to face the nine-headed Lernaean hydra, a great serpent with many heads, whose blood, breath, and scent were poisonous. I had nurtured it on Samos before releasing it into the wild. Since then, it had made its home in the lake of Lerna, hiding in a cave within a spring called Amymone.

After discovering it, having protected his mouth and nose with a cloth from the scent of the hydra, Herakles first shot at it. However, that failed. So he managed to strike off one of its heads with a sword, but two more grew back in its place. And so, with the help of his nephew, Iolaos, they used a torch to burn the neck stump of each decapitated head before it could regrow.

In my determination that Herakles would fail, I sent a great crab to prevent their victory, its claws stabbing Herakles's legs so his wounds might become infected by the venom of the hydra. However, Herakles trampled it under his own foot. Then he finally killed the hydra by removing its final head and, as it was wriggling, put it under a rock so it could not find the rest of its body, for then the monster would rise again. Before he and Iolaos fled to safety, Herakles coated the heads of his arrows in the hydra's blood.

Dismayed at their success, I immortalised the bodies of both the hydra and the crab in the starry sky of Nyx above.

For his third trial, Herakles was to capture the Keryneian hind, the golden-horned, bronze-hooved deer sacred to Artemis, which was swifter than any arrow. I had every confidence it would exhaust the hero. For a whole year, Herakles chased it. Finally, he captured it with nets as it slept. Artemis appeared to Herakles, offended that he had hurt her sacred animal. However, after explaining his situation, she forgave him and let him carry it to Eurystheus.

His fourth trial was to capture the Erymanthian boar, a vicious beast with enormous tusks, and to bring it alive to Eurystheus. He sought the boar in its hiding place, chasing until it was exhausted, and trapping it. He bore it on his back to the king, where he laid it before Eurystheus's throne.

Herakles was proving most resilient, which was infuriating for both me and Eurystheus. I scanned the land for a task so demeaning and impossible that he had to fail. As Helios was shining brightly upon the kingdom of his son Augeus, the idea came to me.

King Augeus owned thousands of cattle, the largest herd known. His stables were filled with the most enormous amount of dung imaginable. The herdsmen never cleaned the stables, fearing that the waste might be poisonous. Eurystheus demanded Herakles's task was to clean the stables in a day. So confident in his ability was Herakles that he even convinced King Augeus to pay him one-tenth of the cattle should he succeed. Then he opened the stable when the cattle were grazing and dug two trenches to divert two rivers to flow in one opening of the stables and out the other to flush out the dreaded dung. Augeus refused to honour their agreement, so Herakles brought the matter to court. Eurytheus banished him from the kingdom and slew Augeus.

The sixth task was to rid the citadel of Stamphalos in Arkadia of the enormous flock of marauding birds that attacked its citizens daily. These were birds who fed on human flesh and dwelled in the nearby lake. Herakles showed no fear as he climbed a nearby hill and made such a cacophony, with a set of clappers, that the birds were scattered by fright into the sky. He shot some down with his poisonous arrows. At the same time, the rest flew away, bringing evidence of his slaughter back to Eurystheus.

After that, Herakles was directed to capture the Kretan bull, the father of the Minotaur. The animal had been rampaging through the island for years, creating havoc, terrifying the locals, destroying crops, uprooting trees and knocking over whatever stood in its way. Undaunted, Herakles quickly overcame the beast, wrestling it to the ground and then leading it back to Eurystheus. However, the king did not wish to have an angry bull in the city, leaving him free to roam.

I admit, by this stage, I was impressed that Herakles never seemed to tire. However, it irked me greatly how Zeus bragged about each success that his incredible son, as he put it, had. So I racked my head for other perils to put the hero through.

Herakles's eighth task was to capture the mares of Diomedes, a Thrakian king in the north who liked to feed his people to his horses. So wild and savage were these beasts they had to be chained down to stop them from escaping. I warned Diomedes, in advance, of Herakles's strength and fearlessness. Diomedes decided to strike at night to cut Herakles's throat, but Herakles had stayed awake, waiting. As they fought, Herakles went to the stables, killed Diomedes and fed him to the mares. Herakles brought them back, and Eurystheus dedicated them to me and then set them free.

Next, I sent Herakles to a woman. Not just any old wench but Queen Hippolyta, daughter of Ares, and mighty in her own right. She was the Queen of the Amazons, the horde of she-warriors who rejected Hellenic customs and the lives of their women. I had often admired their strength and way of life — they kept their husbands and children entirely separate from themselves, only going to them when it was time to procreate, leaving them to raise the girls and kill the boys.

Herakles was told he had to bring back the belt of Queen Hippolyta — King Eurystheus wanted it for his daughter — which was a piece of armour she wore around her breast which could also carry her weapons. Herakles sailed with companions to their lands. However, he was welcomed among the Amazons as a sign of respect for his rank, to my great shock. They even promised to give him the belt, as he came in peace.

So, I went in disguise among the Amazons, and informed them of Herakles's desire to kidnap their queen for himself. A little white lie, I know.

"Sisters," I addressed them in a call as they gathered around. "I bring terrible news. It gives me no joy to say that a messenger has arrived from Hellas, declaring that Herakles, whom we have let into our lands and honoured with a good reception, intends to kidnap our queen!"

Murmurs of shock and horror echoed among the warrior women. Fierce looks of anger came over their faces.

"We cannot let this foreign rat betray our hospitality like this and dishonour our tribe in such a way!" I called out. "Let us bring him to the sword and make him rue the day he thought to deceive the Amazons!"

It was that easy to rile the women to war. Arming themselves and mounting their horses, the cavalry of barbarian women charged upon Herakles's ship. Realising his position, he ripped Hippolyta's belt from her and her sword from its sheath, slitting her throat, before engaging in battle with the rest of the Amazons and returning home, successful in his quest.

The cattle of Geryon were his tenth task, guarded by the two-headed hound Orthus, cared for by a herdsman called Erytion and owned by Geryon, a Gigante with six arms and three heads. His task was to bring the whole herd back from the island of Eythia, near Iberia, back to Argos. Through the blessings of Helios, Herakles arrived prepared for his task. He killed Orthus and Erytion with his club and the armoured Geryon with his poisonous arrows. Furious, I sent a gadfly to harass the cattle and scatter them so they would be impossible to herd. Then I sent a flood, bringing the sea inland, swelling the river so he could not cross. However, the demigod deceived me by laying down boulders along the river. Through them, he succeeded in his task.

On his way home to Hellas, he met two monsters, Albion and Bergion, sons of Poseidon, and their forces, who attacked him. Still, Herakles prayed to his father, Zeus, for aid. They could not withstand the might of the King of Heaven and his favourite demigod, so my husband and his bastard won the battle. Herakles made his way to the palace of Eurystheus, where he sacrificed the cattle to me.

I appreciated the reverence, and I wondered whether or not to keep my hand from tormenting the hero any further. He had redeemed himself, after all, by completing all ten tasks. Perhaps he deserved my clemency now. But Eurystheus was not ready to end his enmity and strayed from my guiding hand. He decreed that as Herakles had received help in killing the hydra and as he sought payment for cleaning the stable of Augeus, he should do another two tasks.

The eleventh trial was to bring Eurystheus three golden apples, something I never would have desired Herakles to do since these apples came from the Tree of Life in the Garden of the Hesperides near Mount Atlas.

Since inheriting the garden from Gaia, I had noticed that the Hesperides, sweet and attentive as they were, often could not resist climbing the Tree of Life and taking its fruit for their own bellies. To prevent overconsumption, I had placed a dragon called Ladon, a son of Typhon and Echidna, within the vast tree branches to guard the apples.

When I realised that Herakles's tasks had taken him there, I had discovered this too late, with Zeus once again bragging about it over breakfast, and how the whole world now knew of my garden, my secret sanctuary. Wondering frantically how Herakles had found its location and how Eurystheus had known of it too, I bolted from Olympos. Upon later reflection, it seemed to me that Eurystheus had heard of the existence of the golden apples, but not necessarily that they came from the Garden of the Hesperides.

To my dismay, I found the gates smashed into rubble. On the other side, the Hesperides were cowering in fright amid the shrubs and the slaughtered body of the great Ladon lying at the foot of the Tree of Life, which was now bare of good golden fruit, the blood over its white branches, seeping from the dragon's corpse and polluting the entire garden before my sight, for death in the Garden of Life was a crime above all others. With this, the tree was rotting, the streams clogged with Ladon's ichor, and the leaves had withered. Bodies of wildlife were strewn over the grassland, dying, for they, too, had drawn their life from the tree.

Rage filled me, and my vision blurred as I returned the body of Ladon to the Underworld. I willed the air from the sky above to descend so it could fill the lungs of the animals and bring them back from the brink of death. I prayed to Eos, the Dawn, for her light above to be soaked into the tree's leaves. Gradually, the Tree of Life started to heal.

After helping the Hesperides recover from their shock and drain the rivers of blood, I removed my counsel and favour from Eurystheus's side, disgusted with him for setting such a task to Herakles but not before inspiring him with a genuinely impossible request to make of the hero for his twelfth labour. Whatever clemency I had been inclined to show Herakles was eradicated after his destruction of my garden.

Finally, Herakles learned he would be set free from his labours if he brought back Kerberos, the three-headed hound guarding the gates of the Underworld. With this task, he would surely die at Kerberos's claws and be shut inside the realm after conceding to consume the food there to sustain his life. Either way, I was sure to be victorious.

I did not bring myself to watch this one as I had no desire to return to Haides's kingdom. Nothing could ever compel me to return to that dreaded place. But it was only after I had heard he successfully entered the Underworld that I heard reports of gods who had helped him get there. It seemed that Zeus had rallied support for his son from amongst the rest of our family. I should not have been surprised, and it made me feel isolated. Apparently, Haides was most accommodating: Herakles could take Kerberos if he only used his strength to tame the beast. And so, Herakles once again wrestled the monster to the ground and brought it back to Eurystheus. I never said he was the most imaginative hero. At last, he was free to go as long as he returned Kerebos to the cave, which he did. Eurystheus gave in to his weakness and bitterly let the demigod go free and redeemed.

Infuriated, I cursed every name I could think of, starting with Zeus for begetting the bastard in the first place. I resolved that I would have my revenge against Herakles one day.

21: GIGANTOMACHIA

The Alodae brothers, Otus and Ephialtes, were twins, sons of my brother Poseidon from when he impregnated a woman called Iphimedia with his sea foam, which is not an analogy. Once born, the Alodae grew incredibly quickly and to such an enormous size, nine fathoms tall to be exact, that even though they were demigods, they associated with the Gigantes, Gaia's and Ouranos's children, born from Ouranos's ichor falling to the earth when his son Kronos had scythed off his genitalia. They lived in the depths of the sea and land, dwelling under mountains and caverns. Yet the Alodae were beautiful beings, so the danger of being in their presence was somewhat dulled at first sight.

Or at least that was the conclusion I drew when the dark head of Ephialtes appeared over the Olympian mountainside beyond the courtyard outside my bedchamber. I saw him from my bed as I got up for the day. I was shocked and hypnotised at the same time by how sharp and handsome his facial features were. I did not stare when his bulging arms hoisted himself onto the patio or when he stood up to his full, imposing height. My heart did not quicken considerably when his sea-green eyes made contact with mine, and a smirk flitted over his plump lips. I was already petrified, frozen on the spot.

Ephialtes bent down on one knee, making the floor shake. He reached out one massive hand, pushed through the wall, and grabbed me.

The wind rushed against me, and I flailed, unable to scream. I saw the blue and white blur as Ephialtes stood again, bringing me up with him. When he stopped moving and I had a chance to understand what was happening; then my heart began to race. I desperately tried to push his fingers apart to let me go. However, it was no use. He was so much more enormous than I could ever possibly hope to win against.

Suddenly an arrow pierced his cheek. Ephialtes winced and roared, a noise that shook the walls, spit flying everywhere; I was doused in it, head blown aside. It stank of rotten fish and decaying flesh. I nearly threw up, but there was no time as a second arrow shot into his wrist, and he let me go.

Falling through the sky, I landed among the willow tree branches in the courtyard below and then toppled down into the water beneath. Bursting up for air, I took a mighty gasp. Then I opened my eyes.

Ares was flinging spears and shooting arrows without respite at Ephialtes. The missiles were lodging in the monster's skin but were not doing any real damage.

He shouted at me, "Mother, are you all right?"

"Yes!" I cried out, unsure if he could hear me over the Gigante's great roaring.

Suddenly Ephialtes appeared to have had enough of the onslaught and grabbed hold of Ares before toppling down the mountainside.

Scrambling out onto the paving, I screamed out Ares's name. I rushed to the edge.

The two hurtled to the ground and slammed against the earth below, the pounding reverberating for leagues around. Such was the impact the earth trembled and quaked. Ephialtes was barely injured from the fall. Yet Ares, I saw as I watched from my height above, lay unmoving, flattened on the ground. Screaming out his name once more, I felt my panic rise. Then Ephialtes rolled over, snatched Ares, got to his feet and ran away into the countryside of Hellas.

Bolting into the palace, I was not the only one in hysterics. The whole court was in mayhem. As I later learned, Ephialtes had attacked Olympos with his brother, Otus, who had explicitly made his target Artemis. They had tried to storm the palace to rule together. Each wanted to take their favourite Olympian goddess for their queen. Still, they both failed through the tactics of Ares and his brothers and, in the process, carried my son away.

Zeus ordered a search by his fiercest Olympians for our eldest, as the exact location of the Gigantes was unknown. Mountains were scaled, caves explored, stones overturned, every corner of land scoured, or so it seemed, but still no sign.

Through his cunning, Hermes discovered Ares was being held captive in a great bronze jar, known as a pithos, from which he could not escape. Thus, an attack was launched upon the Gigantes. Hermes reported back to the Olympian court how, amid the battle to rescue Ares, Artemis changed into a doe and jumped between the two monstrous brothers. When they tried to shoot her down with spears, they accidentally shot each other.

I cannot speak more about what happened, as I was stuck at home. While my children went off to help find their brother, my sisters and friends consoled me. I waited for more than a year for Ares to return. I was stuck indoors, useless and distressed, unable to help him. It was one of the worst torments I had ever suffered. Even Demeter admitted that though a child being taken from a parent is always torture, at least when Persephone was taken from her, she could leave to search for her.

If something had happened to Ares, I would have been unable to go on. He was my firstborn, the first to give me any fulfilment in my life. I don't know how I would have lived without that constant reminder of his smiling dimples when I saw his children running around the palace. I could not bear it.

So, when he returned, I ensured I was the first person to see him again. I threw my arms around him so he knew I had missed him terribly. I made sure that he knew he was my favourite child. I was not ashamed to admit such a thing after he wrapped his arms around me and cried onto my shoulder.

Zeus had always feared an insurrection, whether from his own children or another race of gods and now it was here. He had been trying to create the Golden Age, an era of peace, prosperity, and perfection where nothing went wrong, and no one saw any need for regime change. Yes, he had suffered a few setbacks, such as our rebellion, but that was long over. The avoidance of the loss of his power and prestige had been the primary focus of his governance. He introduced laws to create a stable society and economy across Hellas. He had given rulers to people without them. He had a large family to prove his legitimacy and bolster his authority. He had let his children have almost free reign over their spirits and desires so long as they did not ignore or disobey him. He had created the illusion that all was well in Olympos and Hellas, and nothing needed to change. However, not all saw it that way, namely, those who had been excluded from this great dominion he had created for himself.

Those were the Gigantes, children of Ouranos and Gaia, monsters of great size and strength, who had been joined in their ranks by other creatures of enormity. Lingering under the earth's surface, for all monsters favoured the darkness, the Gigantes had been multiplying, procreating with each other. Their king was Eurymedon, but their battle champion was the greatest of them all: Typhon, my own son, gifted to me from

Kronos, whom I had born in secret and given to Python all those years ago.

In the aftermath of the capture of Ares, Olympian relations with the Gigantes quickly deteriorated, as one can imagine. Zeus did not take kindly to the kidnapping of his eldest son. We stupidly remained on our mountain and did not disperse so we would be harder to exterminate. Athene had advised such a move, but Zeus felt that we must face a threat together in our place of power. He believed our victory would be all the sweeter and more symbolic.

So, I invited the citizens of Olympos to take refuge there with us. The women and children, who had no experience in battle, were holed up in the palace. Hestia, Demeter, Aphrodite, and I took care of them. For a time, we believed that we might as well have welcomed them into their own tombs. I was particularly fearful for my sons, although I knew Ares could probably take care of himself. Hephaistos, on the other hand, had no military training at all. That useless witch Thetis had given him no such education. When I had bid him farewell before he had gone searching for Ares, I felt like I was dropping him off the edge of Olympos again.

"You are being silly," Aphrodite scolded me, waving my worries away. "Gods cannot die. He will be fine."

"No, but they can be maimed and disabled," I argued. "Hephaistos already is."

The gods made battle plans for the next onslaught as the goddesses and nymphs worked to build our stores of food supplies, medicines, and bandages.

By this point, Herakles was dead.

After completing his labours, he travelled to Ochelia in Thessaly to win the hand of Iole, a princess, as the prize in an archery competition against the king and his sons. Herakles prevailed, but the king feared Herakles would murder Iole and her children, as he had Megara, and reneged on his promise of his daughter's hand in marriage. Iole's brother Iphitos was the only family member to support the match. Still, Herakles, in his fury, stole twelve of the king's mares out of spite. Iphitos sought out Herakles to have the horses returned, but Herakles threw Iphitos to his death over the city wall. So, the Oracle at Delphi obliged Herakles to serve penance which this time was under Queen Omphale of Lydia for a year.

While at the Lydian court, he was forced to live with the female servants, do their work, and wear their clothes, while Omphale donned his Nemean lion skin and carried around his wooden olive club. During this time, Herakles showed no rancour nor any heroics, except he killed a man called Syleus, who used to make every passerby dig in his vineyard, and then Herakles set it on fire. After the year was up, Omphale liberated Herakles but then married him. I found it fascinating that he agreed to be the husband of a woman who had dominated him for a year and would consistently rank higher than him. Herakles, the manliest of men, the epitome of masculinity, served and was dominated by a woman. No one could understand it. There were rumours of a son born shortly afterwards. Still, as Herakles remarried a few years later, I presume Omphale died, maybe in childbirth.

Then Herakles moved to Sardinia, and there he made sons, whom he had sired from the daughters of Thespios, the founder and leader of Thespiae in Boeotia, in mainland Hellas. Thespios married Megamede, and the poor woman gave him fifty daughters. But, bizarrely, instead of finding them all happy marriages from which he could have grandchildren, Thespios settled on Herakles as his only choice to keep his line alive, on condition the hero Herakles killed a particular lion for him. The hunt for the lion lasted for fifty days, and during the nights, Herakles slept with each of Thespios's fifty daughters. Thespios did not even wait for the lion to be caught and killed. That was how much mortal men adored the hero Herakles.

Stories abound about Herakles and his heroics. Some say he joined Iason's crew, the Argonauts, on their mission to get the Golden Fleece, but this would have been impossible as Iason's time was before that. Recall that it was my meeting with Medea which spurned my hatred for Zeus's mistresses at the time when the gods were still being born. No, Herakles's fame stretched so far and wide that for centuries to come, authors, poets, and songwriters would insert him into every myth they could think of, into canonisations of the original stories.

Then came the beginning of Herakles's end, the day when he fell in love with a princess of Kalydonia, Deianira. She was also wooed by the god of the River Acheloos, the largest river in the land. The god changed into a bull and attacked and wrestled Heracles but was defeated. Herakles took Deianira as his wife. He and Deianira fell in love, and having had his fill of bloodshed and war, Herakles envisioned retirement, so the couple attempted to go to Tiryns, where they could settle down. On their travels, they had to cross a rapid river. A centaur called Nessus appeared and offered to carry Deianira across while Herakles swam. Agreeing to the kind offer, Herakles took off across the river. Still, Nessus, being the typical crafty centaur he was, attempted to kidnap Deianira instead. Herakles heard her screams and shot Nessus with his poisonous arrows before swimming back to her. As he did, Nessus apologised to Deianira. He gave her his tunic, soaked with hydra blood, telling her it had magic which could excite her husband's love if she ever feared him growing weary of her. Deianira gratefully took the tunic.

This was my opportunity, and with no great effort required. Not long after they reached Tiryns, rumours told Deianira that another woman was vying for Herakles's hand at my orchestration. Remembering the tunic, she gave it to Lichas, a messenger, to give to Herakles. When he donned the tunic, the hydra blood began to burn. His skin felt on fire as it melted down his skin to bones and organs. Thinking it was a trick of Lichas, Herakles hurled him into the sea, where he turned into a rock. Then Herakles built his own funeral pyre from trees. He uprooted himself in agonising pain, and his friend Philoctetes lit a flame, sacrificing Herakles. Philoctetes then collected the arrows, still soaked in hydra blood, and would later take them for his weapons in the Trojan War. As the body of Herakles burned away, the flames overwhelmed the pain of the hydra blood. Zeus sent his great golden eagle to douse Herakles in ambrosia and bring his immortal soul to Olympos, deifying him. For Zeus, as sad as he was to see his son's mortal life end, he was elated to finally have Herakles beside him, not least as he needed him to fight in the ongoing war against the Gigantes, for as the prophecy went: the Gigantes would never be defeated unless the Olympians had the help of a mortal.

Herakles was in my home, with pride of place by his father, part of the family — but not mine. It frustrated me that all my planning had ended up with him in my home. Despite succeeding in killing him through his wife's will, I didn't think I could ever live with him in peace.

As always, the Moirai had other plans.

The Gigantomachy truly began when one of the most potent Gigantes, Alkyoneus, stole the cattle of the great sun-god Helios. Herakles and Athene set off to battle in his homeland of Pallene, where he had fled. Wisdom and strength, Zeus said. While not pleased Herakles had been selected over Ares, I secretly wished them success. Athene told me what happened: Zeus ordered Eos not to rise and Helios and Selene not to shine. In the darkness, Herakles and Athene rounded up the cattle and attacked the sleeping Alkyoneus. Since Alkyoneus remained strong while his feet touched the ground of his birth, Herakles lured him away from his native land and defeated him. Both Athene and Herakles returned to battle, where Herakles aided Apollo in the slaying of Ephialtes, both men shooting an arrow into each Gigante's eyes.

The next day, burning trees and boulders showered down upon Olympos from on high, a terrifying spectacle. The Gigantes launched them as missiles from far away. For a moment, the resentment I felt for this place subsided. I remembered all our hard work in building the city, this place we called home. Heaven was being razed to the ground. Olympos was nearly destroyed.

Hermes related news of the battle to us stuck inside, retelling the horrifying scenes and gruesome sparring between the Olympians and the Gigantes. He recounted how Triton, the sea lord under Poseidon's command, blew his shell, scattered the enemy with the terrible noise, and deafened them. The mules that the sirens and satyrs rode into battle, summoned by Zeus to aid the struggle, let out a braying cacophony on the battle charge, adding to the mayhem and shrill battle cry. It unnerved the Gigantes, who had never heard such sounds before. Apparently, some scattered with the noise, terrifying them. However, the monsters regrouped and retaliated fast, setting a dragon on the tail of Athene, who, endowed with strength, grabbed it by its scaly neck and flung it into the sky where, dying from the speed, it joined the stars above.

That was when Hermes announced that Hephaistos stopped him in his tracks after destroying the Gigante Mimas with red hot metal missiles from his forge. Then overwhelmed by the attack, Hephaistos fainted on the battlefield. I jumped to my feet in terror for my poor son. However, the messenger god reassured me that Helios had carried him away in his chariot and said Hephaistos would rejoin the fight when he roused. Aphrodite blushed in shame at her ex-husband's weakness.

Meanwhile, Poseidon, having chased Polybotes over the sea surface, used his trident to lift up some of the islands and hurl it at the Gigante, blowing his head open.

Hermes relayed his victory against Hippolytus, grabbing him by the hair and slicing him through with a sword. He also told of how Artemis felled Gration with her bow and arrows, swiftly shooting them in rapid fire, so there was no escape.

Then he recounted how the Moirai, abandoning the palace cowards, left the city, hobbled down the mountainside and joined the gods in battle, choosing to help their destiny instead of the Gigantes. Appearing from behind the forest trees, they picked up fallen branches, set them on fire with their magic, turning them into bronze clubs, and, surprisingly spritely for a trio of crones, beat Agrius and Thaos until they fought no more.

Meanwhile, Athene pursued Enkelados to Sicily, where they speared him and whipped Pallas until he could no longer stand. The goddess of magic, Hekate, attacked Klytios with torches, burning him alive. At the same time, Dionysos used his sacred thyrsos to beat Eurytus. Zeus obliterated many of the rest of the Gigantes with his thunderbolts.

It is said we killed the Gigantes, but that cannot be — they are gods — but so great was their humiliation that their army was destroyed. They have never risen up against the Olympians again. Still, two potent players remained, yet to show themselves: Porphyrion and Typhon, my son. Let me recount the tale of Typhon first.

22: TYPHON

Rumour had it that my son Typhon would become their king if the Gigantes won. He was more prominent and substantial than all the Gigante children of Gaia, with such mass that he was taller than the mountains. His head seemed to reach the stars above. One hundred dragon's heads came from each of his hands, breathing fire out into the air. Below his thighs were vipers coiled around his calves, and when they unravelled, they were as long as the rest of his body up to his head, and they spat venom when they hissed. Upon his back, he bore massive wings, which, when they flapped, caused hurricanes. A wild mane of hair streamed from his scalp and cheeks. Fire flickered in his eyes. Hurling great flaming boulders, he broke out from the earth and made for Heaven, blowing tremendous fire from his mouth. Hermes reported that when some gods saw him, they fled, turning into various animals and birds, some even bolting as far as the land of Aegyptos.

Standing in the courtyard outside my bedchamber, I had seen the earth below Mount Olympos split apart, the ground falling into itself. The land teetered, and the significant tremors destroyed everything in the palace. The impact of the marble floors and pillars killed courtiers where they stood. Those who had survived the initial earthquake ran outside the palace walls to see what was happening.

I stood with my family at the front of the palace, behind Zeus. We all looked down from the heights of Heaven. We saw a monster crawl his way out, opening up the earth behind him into a mighty chasm, scrambling his way up through the lightless pit of Tartaros, lumbering through the Underworld, breaking through the rocks above separating realm from realm and leaping into the light. Then he stood, reaching his full height and seeing the vastness of the universe for the first time in his life. It was the most terrifying spectacle I had ever seen.

Typhon towered over the world, even Olympos, his massive head standing between us and the light of Helios. He scanned the mountain and all upon it. The gaze of each set of dragons' eyes and vipers' rested momentarily on me.

As I looked back at him, terror filled my soul, and the hair on my skin stood on end, telling me to bolt. Yet I did not, for there was something in the way he looked at me that gave me courage. It was a wariness, a confusion.

He glanced between Zeus and me, dividing his attention between us both.

I realised Typhon did not know what to do with me. The rest of the gods he could crush without a moment's hesitation. Zeus, he would tear limb from limb. But his own mother?

I found strength in this and stood my ground. I glanced at the back of Zeus's golden head as he stared at his would-be usurper. Then, looking back at Typhon, I heard myself whispering on the winds to myself, "I am your mother. Of all my children, it was you who I prayed for, a child stronger than Zeus. Show me, Typhon, what I bore. Show my husband how strong you are. Then bring me his body."

No one around me seemed to hear. I could not even be sure Typhon did or that he would have understood me. Yet the Gigante's gaze darkened as he glowered at his nemesis, the King of Olympos. Then there was the loudest roar ever made, resounding throughout the land, numbing and disorientating to any who heard it. It killed birds in the air, stripped trees of their leaves, skinned animals of their fur, and shook the earth's ground. Typhon attacked Mount Olympos.

Zeus did not run from his archenemy. He filled himself with rage, radiating strength and might as he transformed into this gargantuan being, a fearsome beast, broader than all the mountains, soaring up to confront his adversary. I had never known he could achieve such a presence. He had never looked so powerful. The world fell into torment from the energy unleashed by his power. Winds stormed and whirled and lifted the earth and all upon it. The oceans rose in colossal waves, raging and crashing and flooding the land below. It was as if the whole world was seething, incensed and indignant at this attack.

The battle for supremacy in the cosmos began. Zeus sent down firebolts from on high, burning Typhon, and attacked him head-on with a sickle, wounding him gravely. Typhon fled, with the earth shaking as each enormous leg pounded the ground. Then he ascended into the air, his wings propelling him eastward, adding to the turmoil around him. Zeus hunted him over the dark Great Sea.

They disappeared from our sight, but as Zeus would have it, they wrestled upon Mount Casius, Zeus caught by Typhon's snakes as they slithered up his body, pulling Zeus in closer, sweeping and sneaking around him, squeezing, and tightening with every breath Zeus took. Then in a mighty breath and concentration of mind, Zeus expanded his form to break the venomous ties. Then freed, scorched by the fire of the dragon heads, Zeus took his golden sickle and swiped them clean off. He wrapped the Gigante's hands tightly with chains, crushing his flesh. But Typhon mustered his mighty strength, shattered his shackles, and tackled the sickle from Zeus. Then they used their teeth and nails to bite, pierce, and slash each other as Zeus desperately fought to take his sickle back.

Before he knew it, Typhon slashed the sinews of Zeus's hands and feet before lifting him on his shoulders, running out to sea, and imprisoning Zeus in his home in a Korykian cave on Sikilia. Zeus was left unable to move, crippled. Typhon set the half-dragon woman Delphyne to guard him and the severed sinews, which he hid in a bearskin, as he made his way back to destroy his remaining enemies on Mount Olympos.

Hermes had followed. Having distracted Delphyne, Hermes returned the sinews to Zeus, who transformed into a bird and returned to Heaven. Wasting no time, he rode back down Mount Olympos on his golden chariot of pegasi and rained more lightning bolts down on Typhon.

Zeus chased him to Mount Nysa. The Moirai had tricked Typhon into eating ephemeral, convincing him that the white flowers contained unique nectar to strengthen him. Instead, they made him weak. Typhon struggled while Zeus gave chase. They stopped to fight in Thrake, Typhon picking up mountains and flinging them at Zeus, who shot them back with his lightning. The valley was filled with Typhon's blood, and the mountain was called Mount Haemus thereafter.

Tired and weakened, Typhon fled to the sea of Sikili, where Zeus hurled Mount Aitna down upon him. At last, flattened, Typhon drowned, but to ensure Typhon was vanquished, Zeus hurled thunderbolts upon the mountain, and it is said that, to this day, the fires can still be seen.

Did I mourn Typhon? He was of a different species, a race which tried to destroy my own, but I felt sorrow, regret, and shame. While Typhon had not been of my kind, he had been my son. I had wished for him. I had wanted him. He was the only one of my children I had ever asked for — all the others were a consequence of either rape or infidelity. It was a great pity that I had to give him away. I briefly wondered what it would have been like to raise a Gigante, a monster, and love him like my other children. Then I stopped my thoughts. If I had brought the baby Typhon to Zeus, he would have destroyed it. There was no point in wondering what might have been. In terms of motherhood, I made the right decision. It was all the motherhood I would have been able to give him.

However, the Gigantomachy was not over yet. There was still Typhon's heir to deal with. Little did I know that I would be essential to Zeus's strategy to defeat him.

23: PORPHYRION

I believe Typhon had done his best. While his battle with Zeus was over, I knew mine would continue, so I retired to my quarters, sickened by it all. I decided whatever fighting of Gigantes was left, they could do it without me. Entering my bedchamber, I closed the doors, thinking I needed my rest. I could hear the howling, roaring wind, and the earth quaking under my feet. However, no sooner had the doors been shut than they were kicked down, crashing and crumbling to the floor. I turned around and screamed.

A hideous sight stood before me. I had never seen this creature before in my life until that moment when he burst into my quarters. One could not even imagine him in one's nightmares. He was a hairless beast, the colour of night, black-blue, at least twice the size of any Olympian — I could see how he might have overwhelmed forces or slipped past them through the shadows. What alarmed me most, though, was his featureless face. It was so utterly frightening, I could not clearly see any eyes, nose or mouth, just a face of folds of flesh. I will never forget the talons, long dagger-like nails on hands as large as swords at the end of each arm, swinging towards me. Wearing only a loincloth, the beast stomped into my room, looming before me. His eyes were fixed on me.

Terrified, I stumbled back and pressed my back up against the wall.

Lunging forward and growling, a noise so deep it was as if it came from the earth's core, the Gigante snatched me up, his talons clamping around my body.

I shrieked as his hand closed around my lungs. This was it. This was the end.

He tightened his grip and tossed me down on the bed, my back landing violently. He reached to his waist with his other hand to untie his loincloth.

My wriggling was doing no good — his massive hand had me pinned to the bed.

Screaming for all I was worth, I begged him to go no further. "Please, please stop!"

Out of the corner of my eye, I saw Zeus and Herakles appear in the battered doorway, weapons ready.

"Help me!" I shouted.

Then the hulk-of-a-thing dropped his loincloth.

"Zeus!" I yelled. Why was he not moving?

"Now?" Herakles asked, approaching the bed.

"Wait. We need to wait for the right moment," Zeus replied.

"What?" I screeched, tears of terror blurring my vision. "Do something!"

"Father!" Herakles snapped as the creature raised my skirt with his other hand.

Giving up on them, I stopped moving, squeezed my eyes closed and braced myself. There was no point. I would just have to endure it. I do not know why I expected any help from either of them.

Suddenly, I was released! I coughed out the breath that had been restrained. I scrambled across the bed, moving as fast as I could. Looking up, I saw Herakles shooting arrows from the other side of the bed.

The demon stood, bellowing and flailing, his head and chest pierced and bleeding.

"Father, now!"

Zeus, summoning his white lightning from the sky, threw his bolts through the ceiling into the creature's chest, engulfing the monster in white light and then flames. With a final terrible cry he teetered, about to collapse on top of me.

I scrambled away as quickly as possible while he landed on my bed, smashing the frame beneath him and collapsing to the floor. I screamed as it did so, and then, when I glanced back, I saw the monster's face right in front of mine. Up close, the features on his face were no more apparent.

Herakles came over and offered his hand.

I took it, and he helped me to my feet.

"Are you all right, my lady?" he asked.

A wave of nausea came over me. I shook my head. If I had opened my mouth, I would have vomited.

"Well done, son," Zeus praised him. "Did I not say the plan would work like a charm?"

"Yes, Father," Herakles murmured, not sounding as enthusiastic.

I frowned and looked between them. *What plan?*

"We must return to the battlefield and see which giants are left to destroy," Zeus decided aloud, turning away and leaving the room.

"What plan?" I murmured, still dizzy.

"I would not worry, my lady," Herakles said, letting go of me and turning away.

I grabbed his hand, unnerved. "What plan?" I repeated, determined to get an answer.

He sighed and turned to me. He scratched the back of his head. "We knew the Gigantes would be difficult to defeat, with this one, Porphyrion, nearly indestructible in battle. So we needed him to be distracted."

I felt my stomach lurch.

213

"Zeus cursed him so that he would desire you," he said, giving me a guilty look. "So that we could sneak up on him."

Bait. I had been the bait.

"I did not like the idea, but I had no choice." He shook his head apologetically. "But do not despair, my lady. Father would have never let him hurt you."

I blinked at him, comprehending what I had just been told. Then, as his words settled in, I realised that I did not agree. So I just said: "Thank you."

Herakles bowed his head slightly. "It is an honour and a pleasure to protect my queen."

"After everything I have done to you?" I suddenly was unable to look him in the face.

"I hold nothing against you, my lady."

There was nothing I could do now to save face. "Yet, I am sorry."

He hesitated and then said, "I should have stepped in sooner to save you. I am sorry too."

"Well, I am just grateful someone did," I answered. "You have finally earned your name, now with my blessing. You deserve to be rewarded. Tell me what your heart desires."

His eyes widened. "My lady, you honour me. I hope you will consent to what I ask, for I desire the hand of Lady Hebe, your daughter. Since arriving on Olympos, I have seen none fairer nor gentler than her."

My heart warmed and quickened at the thought of my daughter getting married to the greatest hero of Hellas. "It would be my pleasure to join the two of you in matrimony."

A smile lit up his face.

Then I remembered Aphrodite and Ariadne, two women whom I had pushed into a marriage that was not what they desired. I couldn't let such a thing happen again. So, I added: "If Hebe agrees."

He nodded, bowing his head. "Of course, my lady. I shall ask her myself."

I smiled. "Very well. I give you my blessing to ask her. Let me know what she says."

"Boy!" Zeus yelled, calling him from down the hall.

Herakles raised his eyebrows and puffed out his cheeks, a glint in his eyes. Sweeping a deep bow, he took his leave of me and followed after his father.

After they left, I saw Porphyrion's corpse, burned so black and so dry it looked like an enormous charred wood log lying in the middle of my broken bed. While his body was no more, I wondered where his immortal, divine soul had gone. To Tartaros? Or was it still lurking about in this room. My ignorance filled me with fear.

Then I thought of Zeus and the depth of his deception settled into my heart. Was it revenge for the suffering I had imposed upon his favourite bastard? Would he have waited much longer to save me, or would he have simply let Porphyrion have me? I honestly did not know.

24: EUSEBEIA

I stepped on broken marble, lifting my foot and whimpering. I stayed still for a moment, trying to come to terms with all that had happened, but it was more than just about a bleeding foot or an attack by a monster of the dark. It was more than the horror of the war. It was everything. It was my marriage. It was my children. It was my freedom. It was the total lack of peace and contentment inside me. I could not stand it any longer. I dropped to my knees and sat on the floor, too overwhelmed to cry.

I had no idea how long I was there before I looked up and saw Aphrodite staring at me. I gulped, surprised.

"It is over," she whispered, her eyes shining with hope. "The siege has ended. We won. The remnants of the Gigante army have returned to the abyss beneath the earth, and the war is over. Zeus wants to throw a banquet in celebration."

Then she frowned. "What is wrong?"

"I do not feel like celebrating," I mumbled, glancing at my surroundings. I glanced at Porphyrion's smoking remains on my bed. "I need to clean up here."

"That can wait. You should go see your family."

I did not reply. She would not understand.

"Hera, they need you," she stressed.

Then my tolerance broke. "Do you know what just happened to me?" I demanded, snapping at her. I gestured to my bed. "Look at it!"

She bit her lower lip and nodded, glancing at Porphyrion's body.

"Who would do that to one's own wife?" I demanded, my voice breaking.

Her gaze fell. "It was horrible for Zeus to use you as bait, but you were useful to him; you helped defeat a Gigante."

I scowled. "Useful? I do not want to be used, not even for the greater good. I want to be respected so that I am asked for my help, and for my aid to be appreciated." My eyes stung with tears. "But that will never happen."

Aphrodite approached and sat down next to me. "Hera, you have all the time in the world to find contentment and peace, but a mother's duty is never done. Being a good wife and mother is the epitome of devotion, piety, and fidelity; eusebeia. It may be challenging, but you should be proud of yourself," she reminded me.

I took a moment to think about it and sighed. "If that is true, then motherhood and matrimony are promises to live for others. What kind of existence is that?"

She hesitated. "I do not understand you."

I shook my head, frustrated. "I was born the goddess of marriage and motherhood, yet I was forced into being a wife and mother. My family life has been a complete disaster. I have made so many mistakes. Meanwhile, Zeus has broken every vow he ever made to me. How is our marriage still valid? How can I possibly be an authority on these things?"

Aphrodite put an arm around me. "Hera, your children will always need their mother. Her presence, her warm hugs, would be of great benefit to them now. As for Zeus? Whether or not he sees it, he will always need his wife, someone he can rely on, who will be in the wings should everything else collapse, as it did today. They all need you now. Focus on those who love you. A new age will come where you will be content and blessed. Just wait."

When I didn't reply, she turned and left me alone.

On my own, I gazed out on the edge of Heaven, onto Hellas below. I thought of Haides and Persephone, dancing in their twilight halls with radiant, vibrant gems shining like stars around them. I thought of how he had discarded his mistress for Persephone and promised to wait for her to come to his bed. I thought of how Herakles had humbly asked for Hebe's hand, the one to whom his immortal soul belonged. I thought of Imbrasos on the island of Samos, how he had been both my guardian and guide through my exile from Olympos. I thought of true love.

I got to my feet and left my bedchamber. Meeting my family, I hugged them: Ares, Hephaistos, Aphrodite, Athene, Artemis, Dionysos, Hermes, Demeter, Hestia, Hebe, Eileithyia, and Eris. I did not embrace Zeus, for I had thought long and hard before the ashes of Porphyrion on what to do with him and I had come to a small solution.

For so long, I had thought that marriage and motherhood were what Zeus decreed because I was naive, and he was terrifying. Perhaps Zeus thought he knew their nature because he believed himself to always be right — he was the King of Heaven; he was the best; and if he was the best, then he could do no wrong; and as a result, if I was unhappy with him, it was not his fault; I was mistaken or an idiot. Perhaps that is why he had never got rid of me, despite all the trouble I had caused him. However, I was tired of trying to figure him out. It was exhausting. I accepted that I would never know him. All I knew now was that Zeus was mistaken, in me most of all. Whatever impression he had of me, it was wrong, and that was his fault, not mine.

After helping restore the palace to order following the Gigantomachy, I began preparations for the wedding of Hebe and Herakles, for my daughter had gladly accepted the hero's hand in marriage. There was no lack of care or compassion between them. Hebe was lucky: her husband was kind and loving. I put all my effort and devotion into the event. It was the first time I was able to prepare a marriage bed for a daughter of mine.

Upon marrying an Olympian princess, Herakles was invited to sit in at council meetings, his opinion of great worth to Zeus. He got on well with his half-brothers, particularly Ares. As for him and me, we were no longer enemies, having forgiven past wrongs. I was one of the few who preferred to call him Alkaios — to address him as 'the glory of Hera' was a strange feeling.

However, for all that, Herakles was my downfall. My treatment of him made me genuinely notorious. It was impossible for him to be adored without telling the tales of his labours caused by me. And so, we were compared: how he had shown true virtue in his benevolence against all my malevolence; how his loving generosity contrasted to my vengeful, wrathful nature; his calmness against my emotional hysteria. All this, along with my history of punishing Zeus's mistresses, allowed everyone, both mortal and immortal, to conclude that I was indeed evil.

Zeus did nothing to stop the rumour mill. Why would he? People asked if he should find a kinder life partner, more submissive and obedient, to take my place. They saw a good king who had always taken the time to improve his wife and be patient with her. They saw an ungrateful and selfish queen who abused her power.

However, I knew the truth: Zeus was a tyrant — a cruel, vicious, unforgiving, unrelenting, brutal beast on the throne of Heaven; that by becoming the most powerful being in the cosmos, he had become the worst, who expected me to take pleasure and be supportive of his actions, even if it stripped me of my privacy and dignity.

I would not live like this, not for an eternity. I was exhausted from trying to prove everyone wrong and being good. What was there to be good for when the masses saw a villain in me, and Zeus was content for them to see me so? I would be compassionate and kind to those who loved me and cared for me, but only for them. I could find the balance between the Kronos in me and the Rhea. If the world hated me, so be it. I could give them a reason. I could be the villain they wanted. I could wait for Zeus to completely forget I had any will. I just had to bide my time.

The rumours, the cold shoulders, the nightmares, the hauntings of the past, the monsters who dwelled beneath the earth, and being left in the shadows didn't scare me anymore. I was used to them. I would use them if necessary. I would bide my time. I would have an eternity to wait for the ideal moment to strike.

A NOTE TO THE READER

Dear Reader,

Hera's story in this book centres around the development of relationships within her family and how that impacts her. To dive deeper into her identity as an ancient Greek symbol and what this has meant for women in the past and today, this story is not only inspired by well-known myths but also lesser known legends from beyond mainland Greece. Bringing these together to create a narrative about family and identity was a fascinating and fulfilling project. I hope you enjoy reading this book as much as I enjoyed writing it.

As reviews greatly help authors starting out, please leave a rating and review on **Amazon** and **Goodreads**. You can find me **on Instagram** and **X (Twitter)**.

I sincerely hope we meet again in the third book in this series!

Ava

Sapere Books is an exciting new publisher of brilliant fiction and popular history.

To find out more about our latest releases and our monthly bargain books visit our website:
saperebooks.com

Printed in Great Britain
by Amazon